Rosa Mackenzie Kettle

La Belle Marie

A romance

Rosa Mackenzie Kettle

La Belle Marie
A romance

ISBN/EAN: 9783337052560

Printed in Europe, USA, Canada, Australia, Japan

Cover: Foto ©Andreas Hilbeck / pixelio.de

More available books at **www.hansebooks.com**

LA BELLE MARIE.

A Romance.

BY THE AUTHOR

OF

"SMUGGLERS AND FORESTERS," "LEWELL PASTURES,"
"THE EARL'S CEDARS," &c.

IN TWO VOLUMES.

VOL. I.

LONDON:
L. BOOTH, 307, REGENT STREET, W.
1862.

LA BELLE MARIE.

CHAPTER I.

THE quiet-looking village of Lezant, niched in the green hill-side, among the wildest of the Cornish moors, woke up into the strangest activity whenever — as was often the case, forty or fifty years ago — from the grassy heights which appeared to shut the place in from the sea, a foreign vessel might be seen, cautiously rounding the points of the neighbouring inlet. On the longest winter night, lights would sparkle all through the darkness from most of the cottages, seeming as if suspended midway in air, so loftily were they perched on the naps, or rocky banks that overhung the valley. By day the place was tranquil enough, and a stranger might have imagined that its inhabitants had no more thriving and exciting occupa-

tion than tending the sheep on the downs,
or loading the lighters which came occasionally into their port for a cargo of slate.   But
at night, the quay and street were thronged
by people, more especially when the nights
were darkest, and the long boom of the thun-
dering rollers from the Atlantic burst upon
the ear, sounding as if the ocean-waves, instead of breaking on the other side of the
great rounded promontory, were sweeping
beneath and undermining it.

At such times, Lezant was more than
usually alive. The wind roaring round the
sharp angles of the buildings, the wet, slippery pathways, were no impediments to the
numerous   foot-passengers.   Every   small
lighted window glimmered aloft, even while
the population seemed mostly abroad, chaffer-
ing, swearing, gossiping, stopping   up   the
steep, narrow thoroughfare, into which the
innumerable flights of steps, by-lanes, and
alleys, wound their devious way.

The entrance to the inlet was guarded by
bold bluffs of black carbonaceous rock, with
soft green turf crowning their rounded summits.   High up along the polished edges of
the cliff ran the broad seamark left by the
last flood-tide that dashed against it.   Mighty
hawsers lay stretched across the cove, ready
to check the swaying of vessels anchored

alongside of the small, but strongly-built
pier, which, with a few rude accommodations
for landing goods and passengers, and some
marine stores and workshops, constituted the
port or harbour of Lezant. The strength of
the chains and hooks used for fastening boats
at the landing-place showed how stormily the
waves at times set into the estuary.

Most of the houses in the upper village
were very old, and many of them tottering to
their fall; but, close to the water, a new and
more neatly-finished building had lately been
erected. Near this spot a crowd of men and
boys were collected, on a stormy evening of
the month of April, looking at the workmen
engaged in setting up the sign denoting that
the place was intended for the entertainment of the public. The new inn was not
popular at present, but its merits had not yet
been tested. Its situation was certainly more
convenient than that of the dilapidated, in-
commodious structure on the top of the hill,
which had hitherto satisfied the townspeople
and fishermen of Lezant, and would still have
gained their suffrages, if the matter had been
put to the vote.

Outside every door of the houses in the
main street were large bundles of furze and
firewood, brought in and dropped there by
carts from the country. Though the downs

above the village rose high and bare, there
was abundance of timber in the deep hollows
among the hills. The litter on the narrow
strip of side-pavement, formed by round stones
set close together, left hardly any room for
foot-passengers ; while the middle of the causeway was broken up by the transit of heavy
trucks during the winter, conveying slate for
shipment at the then comparatively sheltered
quay.   Two blacksmiths' forges, at which
horses were standing, seemed in full play, and
the high wind scattered the sparks abroad as
they flew from the anvil.

Up this steep, stony street, a party of
three persons, who had just landed from a
boat belonging to a vessel in the offing, proceeded as fast as was possible, considering the
impediments in their path.   One of them was
a female, and she was encumbered by a heavy
boat-cloak and an umbrella, which threatened
to turn inside-out as the gale caught it.
Though she was young and handsome, neither
of her companions offered to assist her, but
she battled good-humouredly with the blast,
drawing her skirts away from the brambles
and prickly furze against which the wind blew
them, and displaying momentarily a very
pretty slender foot and ankle, cased in neat
French boots, much too delicately soled for
the muddy, unflagged pavement of Lezant.

Then, as the refractory umbrella resisted her efforts to manage it, she laughed merrily, shrugging her shoulders with a gesture which was not English, and looking half-timidly, but with eager interest and curiosity, down the dark, intricate passages between the houses, leading to other, still more ruinous, dwellings. Once only she paused, where a wider aperture allowed her, now that she had mounted so high, to get a glimpse of the sea, and of a raking-masted schooner tossing on its waves; her bright, dark eyes filled with tears, and she uttered one soft word in a foreign language, almost under her breath; but, low as it was, the man at her right hand heard it.

" So, you're sorry to leave the schooner, mistress? though you've had but a foul time of it," said the rough, but kindly-natured English sailor, who was mate of the vessel in the offing. " I'd rather by far be at sea, once we get a clear berth for the schooner to roll in, than pitching and tumbling in the ruts and mire of such a place as Lezant. Ugh! what a hill it is! and look at the litter! They're more like pigs than Christians that live here; and hang me, if they were pork, if I'd like to eat them. It's not going to be a pleasant night for travelling through those

dark lone woods that lie along the road
you're bound for. Here is our inn, mistress :
you'd best go in and dry yourself."

He pointed, as he spoke, to a large, rambling stone building, with a deep porch standing out into the road, over the portal of which
three crowns were cut out roughly, in strong
relief.

" I never heard of the Boscawen Arms
before to-night, but we all of us know our way
to the Three Crowns; and I see no need to
set up another tap, when there's such a good
one as Mother Brock's in the place. There
she is, in the door-way! I'll be bound she
don't keep customers waiting, though she
doesn't run after them, singing her own
praises, like those gentry on the quay. Holloa,
dame! here's company to see you. You'll
have to make much of visitors, now there's
such opposition in the town. I'll warrant,
you've seen the schooner's masts already, and
looked for a call from us."

A middle-aged, robust woman, who had
come out into the porch with a light in her
hand, welcomed the men cordially as they
mounted the steep steps up the bank. She
then went nearer to the girl, who hung back,
as if tired and timid.

" Here's this young woman wants to go

to Woods to-night, dame. Is there any conveyance to hand?" asked the mate. "We must look sharp to be aboard again."

"Well, come in, come in! It won't hurt you to warm yerselves, and take a glass of something hot this windy night. It's a long time since I've seen ye, Mr. Mabb," said the landlady, hospitably ushering them over the flags of a stone-paved passage into a large, warm, comfortably-lighted room, which formed the kitchen as well as the tap of the establishment. "Going to Woods, is she, this time of night? That's a queer thing to do! I hope some of the farm-people are coming to fetch her. I've nobody here that would set off on a dark night on such an errand. But never mind, my dear, don't be frightened! Come in, and warm yourself. There's nothing to hurt ye, alive or dead, at the Three Crowns; and you must be cold, coming fresh off the water."

The young girl entered, not without hesitation, the homely abode to which she was invited, and followed the hostess into the tap-room, where several men were drinking. As the colour rose to her face, she looked strikingly pretty. Bright black eyes lit up her dark, but clear complexion. Her hair, which was arranged after a foreign fashion, was very smooth, notwithstanding the high wind with

which she had been contending; and her dress,
though plain, was of French material and make,
as was the silk mantle she wore under the
boat-cloak lent her by her companions.

Mrs. Brock took it from her civilly, and
hung it up to-dry; and the men lowered their
voices, and made room for the young lady to
come to the fire.

" Hang me if I didn't think we'd mistaken our moorings, when I saw a sign swinging close to the water's edge!" said the mate
of the schooner, while Mrs. Brock's face grew
red with suppressed passion. " Why, it's
like a card-house, they've run it up so quick.
Will the walls hold, think ye?"

" Like enough not!" said the hostess,
contemptuously. " There's more mud and
rubbish than stone and mortar in that house.
It must be pleasant to have all the town dirt
stream down the street, right to your door,
when the autumn rains flood the gutters; and
the sea-weed smelling enough to choke ye.
Folks had need to have neither eyes nor noses
that go to a place down in a hole like that,
with the sea-water knee-deep in the cellars.
I'm surprised any one could think of such
folly. We've more custom than ever, since
the Boscawen Arms was opened. It's an
insult to a gentleman's name to set it up
in that way for the boys to laugh at."

" It 's very near all the good my lord 's
ever like to do them. You needn't grudge
the poor devils their fine name!" said a man
drinking at the table, who held a small copyhold farm upon the moor near Camelford.
" What do you take, gentlemen? There 's a
capital tap, and good brandy in the cellars.
I guess I need not tell *you* that," he added,
smiling, and lowering his tone. " Is not that
the schooner in the offing? Will Mynheer
be in Lezant to-night?"

" No, no, he 'll not land! He won't run
our beauty in on such a plaguy night as this
is like to be," said the mate, good-humouredly.
" He 's a tight hand, too, and we mustn't
outstay our time. Give us some ale, hot
and spiced, as Mrs. Brock knows how to
make it. We mustn't stop afterwards; but
the Captain said we were not to lose sight
of the young woman till she was in safe
hands."

" Well, she 's safe enough here," said Mrs.
Brock. " So, Mynheer sets store by her?
There 's not much of the Dutchwoman about
her, but she don't look English. What
country does she belong to?"

" Oh, she 's half English! at least her
mother was, and her name is not a new one
hereabouts. She 's kin to the Jerseyman,
Helier, at the farm down to Woods, and she

is to go there to-night. Some one will be here presently to fetch her."

"Well, it isn't many people travel that road after dark. She'd do well to put up here, and wait till morning. There'll be the butter coming in then. It's market-day to-morrow, and she might go back in the cart. There's no carriage set up yet in Lezant, thank goodness! though the new people talk of keeping one. They'd be wise to see what custom they have before they spend much more of their money. I warrant, they did not count the cost before they began building. Best let ma'amselle sit with my old man till I get her supper. He'll find lots to entertain her with. He's got Scripture verses at his finger-ends, and she looks half a child. 'Twill do her good to listen to him: I'm tired of it. For all his talk of goodness, nothing comes of it: it don't bring grist to the mill. He's not done a stroke of work for nigh upon a score of years, and yet he looks hearty."

The dame pushed back a curtain which hung by rings from a heavy oaken beam across the long room, dividing it into two unequal parts, while at both ends fires were burning. One side was all noise and tumult — the clash of idle merriment;—the other was singularly quiet. An old man was sitting in the chimney-corner, with a small table beside him, on which lay a Bible and one or two tattered hymn-books. He was not reading, but looking into the fire, and every now and then striking the ashes from the bowl of the short pipe he was smoking. In his youth he must have been very handsome and powerfully built, but for many years his right side had been paralysed. The defects of his education made him entirely dependent upon others, in his infirmity, for amusement and instruction; and he was often a sore incumbrance to his brisk, active helpmate.

"Here's a lady to sit with you, Simon! You know how to please the gentry. You can get her to read your books to you, when she's a bit rested," Dame Brock shouted in his ear. The old man, whose hearing was not impaired, seemed confused and troubled by her loud voice and bustling manner; but he half rose as the girl approached, and received her civilly.

She spoke to him kindly, in English, but with a foreign accent and idiom. The old man answered in monosyllables, then both sat silent.

"And now, my masters, what more shall I get you?" the hostess said cheerily, as she went back, leaving the curtain half undrawn, that she might attend to the wants of all her customers.

" Where 's that lazy fellow, Andrew ?   It 's
a good thing there 's one person with a head
on her shoulders and a good pair of legs to
carry her through the day ; the work would
never be done else.   Where 's Andrew, I
say ? "

" Here, mother," answered a great, tall,
soldier-like man, emerging from a sort of trap-
door, with two jugs of foaming malt in his
hands, and stumping across the kitchen as
fast as one stout limb of his own and a wooden
leg would bring him.   " What are you pitching into I for ?   There 's feyther — give it he,
if you want some one to jaw at.   I 'll be
hanged if I stand it.   You may fetch the yale
yerself next time."

He stood sulkily at the table, on which he
had banged one of the jugs ; but he still kept
fast hold of the other, till he reached a great
pewter mug that was hanging on the wall,
filled the measure, and drained it off at a
draught.

" That 's good liquor as ever was brewed !
I 'm ready to wallop the fellow that says the
Three Crowns doesn't give the best of everything that 's to be got for money.   Holloa !
who 's that lass talking to feyther ?   The old
chap knows a pretty face when he sees one.
Stand out of the way, old woman !   I want to
get a look at her."

"Be quiet, Andrew; would you give the house a bad name?" said his mother, her face flushing angrily. "People will say decent folk shouldn't put up at the Three Crowns, if you use such language. The young woman is going to Woods, and wants to be on the road to-night. Are any of the farm-carts in the yard? I don't fancy," she added, with a sneer, "that *you*'ll offer to take her."

The bully turned pale at the thought. "*I* take her through those tarnation woods in the dark? I'd throw her into the Keeve first! What takes her there, of all places in the world? Did she come in the schooner?"

"Yes; Mynheer gave her a passage, poor soul! She has lost her friends," said the mate, in an undertone. "She didn't make no work on board, though we were out in rough weather, and the cabin was too full for us to make her over-comfortable. Nothing tries the temper more than sea-sickness, and getting wet and cold with the salt-water washing over the deck; but she bore it like a good one. I should wish to know she will be in safe hands when we leave her."

"I don't envy any one that has got to put up at Woods," said the landlady. "There's been a power of gentry there lately; all the clergy in the country sent for to lay the ghost; and who do you think they set to do it, but

our poor feckless Parson? People wondered
he chose to go, but I believe it was a silly
bravado. They drew lots, and the longest
fell to him; but he'll never do any good.
Words of power don't fall from his lips; all
his congregation are leaving him. They should
have had the bishop and all his chaplains;
and, even then, if the Evil One takes a fancy
to a place, as he has done to that old house at
Woods, you won't get him out of his snug
quarters in a hurry. There are some places
that never can be made quiet, and Woods is
one of them."

"Don't talk so fast, mother," said Andrew
Brock, uneasily. "We all know who it is that
walks at 'Oods, and Lance Fleming will be
here presently. He mightn't like it, and we
don't want to send customers to the new
inn."

"Hold your tongue, you saucy jackanapes!
Don't name the new inn to me!" replied his
mother. "Mr. Helier is no such friend of
mine; no, nor of Lance Fleming's, for that
matter, and the place is his now. Why
should Lance quarrel with me for my gossip?
I only say what all the country knows and is
talking about.

"Most people believe that there is a ghost
at Woods, and dozens of us have seen it," pursued the landlady, stanchly. "There's some

laugh and some cry out against it, but I never knew any one that slept twice willingly in one room of that old house. To be sure, there are strange things that haunt those deep woods; the owls and the night-hawks screech fearfully; still, if you're not timid, you get accustomed to them, and to the cracking of the old furniture and the wind in the chimneys: but when a man sits up after midnight in a haunted chamber and comes out with his teeth chattering and his hair white, it stands to reason that he has seen what made the flesh creep upon his bones. I'll be bound for it, the Parson said his prayers more from his heart than folks tell me he does in church, when he was put to sleep in the room where that bloody corpse was once laid out."

"Suppose you spin us a yarn, Dame Brock," said the mate. "I've heard, ever since I was a boy, about the noises and queer sights at Woods, and been shy of the place myself when we've anchored in the creek, and had to carry Lord knows what through the bushes; but no one could tell exactly how the house got its bad name. Was not a foul murder committed there?"

"Murder! Yes, that's the word! If ever there was a man who came foully to his end, my masters, it was the last tenant of Woods," answered Mrs. Brock. "There was plenty of proof; more than enough to hang the murderer, as he would have swung for it, if he had been one of our poor devils lifting a keg through the woods, and in the dark, perhaps, —with a little too much brandy to carry, his hand unsteady, and the stars dancing before his eyes — provoked to strike the man that comes upon him and would take him off to prison, or on board a man-of-war — strikes him, I say, a blow that cuts deeper than he thinks for. If there wasn't other sign of guilt, I'd read it in that poor frightened woman's face —she that is another man's wife now, but was brought home to Woods first by Lance Fleming's father. I tell you, there *was* murder, and she knew it, and swooned away in court when she should have given evidence. She was young and pretty then, and people were sorry for her; but there were lines in that baby-face of hers that don't come for mere sorrow — seams they are now, that will never wear out of it. If his Reverence did not know the truth before about the crime his brother committed, he got it that night from the ghost!"

The superstitious sailors drew nearer to the lights and the fire; while the old man at the farther end of the room laid his hand upon the Bible, as a soldier might upon his weapon.

"Halt, mother!" said the lame man, impatiently. "That's not a pleasant tale you've hit upon, and hang me if you tell it agreeable! You've drove the old man to his books, and gev me the horrors."

"Let the dame finish her story, you coward!" said the mate of the smuggling vessel. "If she's good enough to tell it, we're not afraid to listen. We've a message from our Captain to give to Lance; and if he's coming here to-night, we may as well wait for him."

The old man and the young girl were now both listening; the one with the curiosity of youth, and some spice of superstitious terror; the other, with that weariness of his own thoughts which the want of all occupation engenders.

"You are welcome to my story, gentlemen, though it's no news to most among you," said the landlady. "I was fresh come to the place in those days, married, like a young fool, to a man old enough to be my father. Well, that's neither here nor there. We must drink our malt as we've brewed it; and I wish mine had been as good a tap as the one I've set before ye!

"Mrs. Fleming was a younger woman than I was, when her husband — he that walks still, though he was laid underground

nigh upon a score of years ago—brought her
to Woods. He was a far-off cousin of Lord
Boscawen's, and had spent his money, 'twas
said, in racing and gaming, till he was forced
to leave the army, and the sale of his commission paid his debts. He came here to
look after the property, and lived at the
Manor-house, which had been unoccupied
for years, by favour of his relations. Mrs.
Fleming was no lady, but one whom he had
married in his wild days : they quarrelled
constantly, and were not happy. Some said
she had jilted a person in her own line of life
to marry a gentleman ; but, however that
might be, she had cause enough for sorrow,
since the lonely ways of the place brought
back all his old·faults, and he used to drink
himself half mad.

" His wife was not much of a companion
for him, no, nor yet a useful, commonsense
body. She was a pretty, childish creature,
and when she came to church, our Parson's
brother, Colonel St. Erme, who was often
down at Lezant, used to pay her compliments
sometimes, people said, over the back of my
lord's high pew in the chancel, ·or when he
mounted her on her pillion at the church door,
behind her half-drunk, sulky husband, or—
when he was too far gone in liquor to bring
her—one of the farm-servants.

"Colonel St. Erme was a fine figure of a man—one of the king's equerries—with powder in his hair, as they wore it then at court, and fine cambric and lace in his cravats and handkerchiefs. He was quite different from any of the people hereabouts—his voice had another kind of sound, and he was always gay and generous, not a bit like our old drone of a minister. I believe, sometimes, when he rode home from hunting, the Colonel called at the Grange, and stopped longer than he should have done. Captain Fleming did not like his visits : they had high words more than once, and people talked more than was pleasant about his wife and the Colonel.

"One day, when Mrs. Fleming and her husband set out for church together, he taunted her so that she cried, and then she said her eyes were red and she was ashamed to be seen, and would go back ; so he swore at her, and let her. Colonel St. Erme was not at church, either, that afternoon—no uncommon thing for him : he only went to look about him, and make the girls forget their books and their manners, staring at his powdered hair, and the rings on his white fingers. He was watched, and was seen sauntering on the cliffs, and then to take a road through the woods in company with the silly woman, who afterwards confessed that she had left her husband to keep an appointment with him.

"Fleming got home sooner than was expected, and a very dark frown came on his brow when he heard his baby crying, and was told by a person he had set as a spy over his giddy wife that she had been seen with the Colonel. I'll warrant he drank deep that evening, though he was alone. He was always moody in his cups, and held himself above the only company he was like to fall in with. Many a poor fellow with a bad wife has found more sociability and comfort in our tap-room than under his own roof. The Grange is a lone place, and on Sundays, the few servants kept to do the farm work were mostly taking a holiday. The housekeeper, who was a steady body, and lives there still, was away on a visit to her friends, and Mrs. Fleming up-stairs with her little boy, when the Captain left the house.

"The next morning his body was found at the foot of the rocks, quite cold and stiff, with the blood congealed that had flowed from a wound in his side, made by the bullet that pierced his heart. I believe, the doctor who extracted the bullet has it labelled among his curiosities at Camelford. All the country was up about it, and when the matter was sifted, and great rewards offered, two men came forward to swear that, going along the church-path on their own errand, they saw in the bright moonlight Colonel St. Erme on the cliff with Fleming, who was very abusive, brandishing his stick in the air as if threatening to strike ; but the Colonel wrenched it from him and pitched it over the brow. It was found afterwards, not far from where the body had fallen, with a bit of the Colonel's rich lace frill sticking to the silver knob on the handle.

"The men had business to perform in a given time, and did not wait to see the end ; but a lad belonging to this town, who was setting a trap for a hare (more shame to him) in the broken ground, heard a cry overhead and something like a shot fired, and he, too, said he had seen the Parson's brother come out of the Rectory-gate, and go straight up to the high cliff, where there is the fine look out over the sea.

"Colonel St. Erme was arrested at his brother's house, and charged with the murder. He was dressing when the men went to take him up, and his travelling pistols, freshly cleaned, lay open in a case upon the table. It came out in evidence that he had ordered his valet to pack his trunks, as he meant to leave Lezant next morning. His counsel wanted to set up a plea for

the Colonel, that he had shot Fleming in self-
defence; but that was not what he said himself. He was as haughty and arrogant when
brought to his trial, as if his life had not been
hanging by a thread; and declared, that after
listening to a few angry words he had passed
on, satisfied that Mr. Fleming was not in possession of his senses, and had left him on the
cliff. There was great interest made to save
him : all his connexions were rich, powerful
people; but the spirit of the country was
dead against him, and the jury found Colonel
St. Erme guilty. He was taken from the
Court-house in a close carriage, that the mob
might not see him; and kept in prison till
his sentence, which they managed to get
changed to transportation for life, was put
into execution. It ought to have been
death.

"Men have swung in chains for a less
matter, as those Sussex smugglers did, Harry
Mabb, on Silver Hill, for killing the gauger.
Yes, and French Jerry, as came with you
once, when you put up here, it was transportation they gave *him;* and what for?—
just a clever trick he played the Revenue lads.
I don't see how folks can expect to sleep
quietly in their beds at Woods, when justice
has not been done. No, and they won't neither! while Fleming's murderer is, perhaps,

making his fortune on the other side of the herring-pond.

"What is the old man muttering? He don't believe the story! No! nor more, he won't, and wouldn't if he'd seen it with his own eyes, so long as Mary St. Erme told him it was not right to credit it. She is more than his lost senses to him — more than wife or son! Of course she denies it. She is the murderer's daughter."

As his wife uttered Mary St. Erme's name, the old man's face changed. His countenance lighted up, and he half raised his once powerful frame, as though the bright angel whose presence at times stilled the hot fumes of passion in that noisy room were about to enter.

"It's a queer tale," said the mate; "and I'm glad I've not got to sleep in that old bed you speak of, after hearing it. I say, messmate, when is the fellow from 'Oods coming? We ought to be aboard our vessel."

A sharp sound woke the echoes of the street, which had lately become quiet, as a horse's hoofs clattered on the stony pavement, and stopped at the inn-door.

"That's Lance Fleming's bay mare. Have done with your ghost-stories, mother!" said Andrew Brock, roughly. "You've got a long one in hand to-night, and we've had more than enough of it."

He stumped across the kitchen, as if to greet the new-comer, but, changing his mind half way, stopped, and busied himself with removing the disorderly array of mugs and platters upon the table, just as young Fleming entered.

The son of the murdered man at Woods was at least half a head taller than any one, except the old landlord, in the tap-room of the Three Crowns. If he had not stooped, he would have struck his forehead against the edge of the stone lintel of the door-frame; but the place and its ways were quite familiar to him. Nevertheless, there was about his air and person more than one distinguishing mark that he was superior to the class with which he chose to associate.

There were faces not unlike his, with features finely cut, and even delicate, among the portraits of Lord Boscawen's ancestry that hung in the gallery at Woods. Those faded heirlooms, damp and mildewed, bore a decided resemblance to the handsome youth, who was, indeed, distantly related to the Boscawen family; but Lance was strong and active, accustomed to hardy and somewhat lawless pursuits, and could pull an oar when the black rocks of his native coast were white with the foam that flew over them from the Atlantic. In dress and manner he was a Cornish yeoman, with a dash of the sailor.

He did not notice Dame Brock or the younger woman, but went straight up to the seamen belonging to the foreign vessel, who both stood up, and, in their own independent fashion, saluted him respectfully.

"Does Mynheer intend to land to-night? Has he brought anything for me?" he said, rapidly. "What is your freight?"

"A richer one than a prudent man like our skipper would risk on Lezant quay, now that there are new faces at the waterside public. Times are altered, and we must trim our sails as the wind blows," said the mate. "There's a young woman bound for Woods, and she wants to get along to-night. The rest of the cargo can wait."

Lance lifted his usually downcast eyes, which were shaded by long dark lashes, and cast a shy glance at the girl, who, weary and disheartened, remained quietly seated by the old man, gazing, like him, silently into the fire. Though there was nothing repulsive in her appearance, the young man's glance did not rest upon her for more than a moment. He was quite unaccustomed to the society of ladies, yet he saw immediately that, simple as was her dress, his step-father's kinswoman was of a gentler stamp than his own mother and sisters.

Apparently, this conviction did not set him at his ease. He said, coldly,—

, "She had better go on at once. There is a cart in the town now. I expected something to be landed from the schooner. I will tell the driver to call here."

Then, turning again to the seamen, who were now regaling themselves at his expense, he questioned them, in a lower tone, respecting the chances of their late trip, and their plans for effecting a landing.

"The Curlew will be in our waters next week," he said. "Yes, or even sooner. She has a new officer, and left Milford Haven for Swansea ten days ago. With this wind we may look for her at any moment."

He did not see the girl bend forward to listen, or the bright colour that mounted to her cheek as he spoke.

"Aye, aye, let her come! It's not the first time we have given her the go-by," said the sailor. "'Tis true, she's got a fresh officer, and new brooms sweep clean; but La Belle Marie has a captain that does not sleep at his post!"

"I must see Mynheer to-night," said Lance, as the men rose to leave the inn. "Good night, Dame! Shall I bring you a silk dress or a Lyons shawl? Both are to be had on board La Belle Marie."

. He went out into the street, in earnest

talk with the sailors. Dame Brock now busied herself with the young foreigner, persuading her to take some of the refreshment which had stood untasted before her, and lending her a good warm cloak for the cold night-journey.

At last, the wheels of the light cart grated upon the stones, and the girl, though tired, sprang up, eager for any change of quarters. Nevertheless, it was with a sinking heart that she saw the lights of the village, one after another, disappear, and found herself travelling slowly, along the dark country roads, towards the old Manor Farm called Woods.

CHAPTER II.

REINE HELIER's temper was a cheerful one,
and she shook off the superstitious terrors
aroused by Dame Brock's imperfectly-under-
stood narrative before she had proceeded a
mile upon her way. Sometimes, indeed, she
started at the white ghostly patches of moonlight falling on the stems of the beeches in
the hollows, and listened uneasily to the wail
of the streamlets imprisoned in the labyrinth
of bushes. Then, as the wind rushed wildly
over the barren surface of the Cornish moors,
the young French girl shivered and drew her
cloak around her; but she had never, in all
probability, traversed alone and in darkness
so desolate a country. There was enough to
chill her in the thought that she was an
orphan, and must find a home far from her
birth-place, and among strangers.

The rude vehicle in which she was travelling was open in front and at the back, with a
covering overhead. The driver sat on a plank

laid across the cart, at the farther end from the corner Reine occupied, and whence, whenever the skies 'afforded light, she looked anxiously out over the landscape. The shadows of black clouds were driven across it by the hurrying wind; occasionally, rain pattered among the leaves, but she did not feel it; and, in a few moments, the moon came forth again, silvering the wet foliage. Reine liked to watch these changes, and to hear the man speak kindly to his horse, though the dialect he used was so peculiar that she only knew from his tone of voice that the words were encouraging. The hills were very steep, and when the wind met them at the top of the frequent ascents, the animal would stand still, panting, as if scarcely able to contend with the blast. After a kind word or two he went on; the cart jolting and tilting uncomfortably over the stony winding road.

It was in vain that the tired girl looked out again and again for the lights of the house which was to be her abode. Even when the man, who had been walking by the side of the horse up a steep rise, pointed with his whip down an almost precipitous declivity, Reine could perceive nothing. The trees seemed to close in there more densely than in any other direction, and not a spark gleamed through the thicket. She heard plainly enough his

brief communication that yonder was the turn
to 'Oods; but no change of position could
enable her to see anything resembling a
habitation.

At last it struck her that what she had
been taking for the tops of tall trees were the
high clustered chimneys of a house. There
was no curl of smoke visible against the grey.
sky, nor did the red light of fire or candle
gleam from the windows. But now that she
was close upon it, Reine faintly discerned
the walls and gables — almost as much covered
with ivy as a wood in summer with its leaves
—of the Manor Farm, tenanted by Mr. Helier.
Now that the trees in general were bare, the
building looked greener than the surrounding
plantations.

A light shone forth, at last, from an upper
window, and Reine fancied that she saw a pale
face taking cognisance of their arrival. The
driver did not go up to the front door, but
turning short off, went round the back of the
house into a spacious yard, begirt with barns
and offices, many of which appeared to be
ruinously out of repair. He leaped down
from his rickety bench, and took out the piece
of wood which formed the back of the cart, for
Reine to get down more easily. Warm light
streamed out now from the door and window
of a kitchen, whence a woman of respectable

appearance came forth and invited her to enter.

She did not keep Reine in the kitchen, but led her through a long winding passage to the part of the old house which was occupied by Mr. Helier's family; warning her by the way of the odd steps up and down, which seemed put there as snares to entrap the unwary. As they went along, with the light the woman carried in her hand flickering in the strong draughts which seemed to come from behind the tapestry, as if it masked unseen apertures, Reine trembled as much with fear as with cold. She would have given all she was worth in the world to be back again in France, or on board the schooner, with the kind sailors and their captain. Even old Simon Brock's nook, screened off from the tap-room, was more inviting than the abode of her unknown kinsman.

Reine lingered behind her companion, at the risk of being left in darkness, to try to get over the inclination she felt to weep. As she stood still hesitating, while the woman, who had preceded her with the light, had her hand on the door of the room to which she was showing her, something or some one rushed past her in the darkness. Her already thrilling nerves vibrated with the shock, and she could not repress an ejaculation of terror;

but it was faint compared with the groan or
gasp of apprehension which issued from the
form she could just see leaning against the
wall.

"Oh, Ciel! Qui es tu?" was uttered in
broken accents of alarm, followed by sighs so
profound that they seemed to betoken bodily
as well as mental anguish.

"It's only the Master. Don't be scared,
Miss!" said the woman, returning and looking sharply round. "Was it you that screamed?
People who live at 'Oods should have stouter
hearts than yours seems to be."

She passed Reine somewhat contemptuously, and went towards the dark figure still
propped against the wall. Her tone of voice
was low as she spoke to him; but the girl
could trace in it scorn, if not loathing. It
was not as respectful as it ought to have been
to her master; but all the people at Woods
regarded Mr. Helier as no gentleman, and
treated him accordingly. Whatever repre-
sentations the woman might make were un-
availing. He remained where he was, and
she came back again, saying, Master had had
a start, and couldn't get over it. He would
be in the parlour presently. He was but
a poor creature, and she hoped Ma'amselle
wouldn't mind his crotchets.

Reine did not reply, and the next moment she found herself in the presence of her hostess and of the young girls, to whom, in return for the home offered her at Woods, it was implied, though not stipulated, that she was to afford some instruction. Mrs. Helier, a pale, nervous woman, received her stiffly; her daughters, as shyly as a couple of wild animals might have done. They shrank into the farthest corner of the large, barely-furnished parlour; from which they emerged slowly, after a time, tempted by the bon-bons Reine had brought for them,

The white face of his wife flushed when Mr. Helier came into the room; and as the colour rose to her thin temples, Reine began to credit the assertion she had heard, that in her youth she had been handsome. There was little trace of beauty now; and none of girlish animation or frivolity in that worn, fretful countenance, seamed with lines of anxious care. Mr. Helier was a dark, foreign-looking man, very much sunburned. His French accent brought tears to Reine's eyes, as he bade her welcome. She declined all offers of refreshment, explaining that she had partaken of some while waiting at the Three Crowns; and, after a brief, embarrassed conversation, she gladly retired for the night.

The young orphan was disposed to make the best of the lot before her; and, with the spring sunshine falling on the old house, unbroken, save by the budding branches of the trees, the home to which she had been transferred with much less care and consideration than a bale of smuggled silks certainly appeared to her under its least disagreeable aspect.

The old Grange belonging to the Boscawens stood nearly at the head of a ravine, stretching upward from the sea, and was backed by the high ground of the moors. Down from the heights came a sparkling, dancing stream, dashing over ledges of slate and granite; of which large boulders were scattered about. The stream was visible for a long way; since no hedgerows bordered the open roads, or broke the free turf of those grassy downs. A wide, unenclosed space, dotted with grazing sheep, and, here and there, a clump of thornbushes near the running water, extended to the north and east of the Manor-house.

When the rivulet entered the woods, though it still brawled and dashed along its pebbly bed, its aspect changed. Dark shadows crossed it; almost impervious gloom brooded over it; and its hurrying, foaming current, was impeded by the growth of reeds and rushes, fostered by the warm damp atmosphere. Yet still there were places, especially now when the trees were nearly leafless,

where it broke out gladly into the sunlight.
Reine did not guess, as she impatiently watched
the swelling buds on the great trees, what
masses of gloomy darkness, when they were
in full leaf, those giant branches cast; and
how much more beautiful the woods were in
the spring, than in their full summer verdure.
She could wander about now as she liked;
but when the brambles grew stronger, and
stretched across from thicket to thicket, those
pleasant-looking openings of paths, which, in
general led nowhere, were choked up altogether.

She had not as yet ventured to any great
distance from the house, and by far the densest
growth of brambly covert was that which filled
the hollow between it and the sea. The young
girls, her cousins, told her in that direction
the woods were impassable; and though she
did not quite believe them, and was especially
anxious to tread this prohibited ground, the
place was as yet so new to her, that she con-
tented herself with exploring the immediate
neighbourhood of the Manor.

The dwelling itself was a large quadran-
gular structure, in the Old English style, surrounded by trees, which rendered it cold and
damp in autumn and winter; but which now,
in fine weather, only cast pleasant, flickering
shades on the grey, ivy and lichen-covered

walls. The offices were very large, including an extensive range of stabling, built long ago by the present Lord Boscawen, who had made the place his residence during the hunting season, and had desecrated, it was said, the ancient chapel, by converting it into a harness-room.

In front, the view was circumscribed by trees, which came so close to the house, that very probably some of the mysterious noises which alarmed the family were caused by the grating of the boughs against the walls. The wide avenue leading from the road to the front-door was full of weeds; and the drive to the back of the mansion, cut up by the farm-carts, sorely needed mending. All that was beautiful about the place consisted in the fine old wood around it, in the picturesque style of the architecture; and, at the time of Reine's arrival, the bright April sunshine falling over everything.

French in her lightheartedness and dexterity, and in the taste which regulated her simple costume, Reine Helier was seated in one of the sunniest windows of the old house, busy at her needlework, and singing merrily. The snatches of melody, interrupted while she was considering how to fold the lappets of the high-crowned Norman cap she was making, went on afresh, like the carol of the birds out

of doors, busily occupied, also, in building
their nests in the old trees about the mansion.
The room was a large one, with some pieces
of quaint wood-carving round the mantel-
piece, and a stag's horns over the door.
Several faded pictures of the Boscawen family
—ladies in straw hats and a sort of shep-
herdess costume—hung on the walls. The
furniture was old and scanty, and seemed
rather to belong to a hall than to a sitting-
room; ponderous oak chairs, with elaborately-
carved backs, a threadbare carpet, covering
only part of the floor, and curtainless windows,
with thick stone mullions, through which the
light fell full on the bent head and shining
tresses of the young girl.

Though she had been only three days its
inmate, Reine, as she sat singing over her
light work, seemed quite at home in the old
Grange. Hers was the very nature to lighten
its gloom; the brave, honest spirit and glad-
some temper that laughed at difficulties, or
set steadily to work to overcome them. Her
recent domestic trials were not forgotten: over
that sunny brow there passed, from time to
time, shadows of regret for the lost—visible
clouds of misgiving about the uncertain future;
but there was nothing of the misty, dreamy,
atmosphere of the North, obscuring Reine's
clear intellect. Her sorrows and trials were

real;—they were not magnified by the medium through which she viewed them; and they were chequered by vivid anticipations of enjoyment.

In spite of her French birth and education, Reine had an obstinate partiality for everything English. The song of the birds in the thicket, the breath of the spring wind, even the dismal tranquillity of Woods, pleased her, because they appeared to her natural to the country in which she was come to reside. There were strong emotions stirring in the young girl's heart, which, even while she sat alone, brought blushes to her cheek, and bright light to her eye, as she looked upon the homely features of English country life, seen for the first time at the Manor Farm in Cornwall.

For some time she was quite alone. The children whom it had been understood that she was to educate, were nowhere to be found. Neither the master nor the mistress of Woods promised to be a sociable companion. Reine was left entirely to her own resources for amusement. She rather liked the feeling of solitude and freedom, so different from the picture she had formed to herself of the life of a dependant. Nevertheless, she looked up brightly when Lance Fleming, whom she not seen since the night of her first arrival, came within view on the road leading past the house towards the stables.

He stopped short on seeing her, and seemed inclined to retrace his steps. Reine's half-saucy glance deterred him from approaching her. In general, the wild girls at Woods, with their frocks stained purple with blackberries or green from kneeling on the grass, ankle-deep in mud, and with dishevelled hair, kept him in little awe; but Lance felt that he was no fitting associate for the foreign-looking damsel, with her carefully-braided locks and daintily-neat apparel. She was busy with her work again, however; and did not look up or take any further notice of him. Lance was no scholar, and hardly understood a word of any language but his own; yet he liked the sound of the light foreign words she was singing. He came in and sat down at the further end of the hall, where it was in shadow.

Reine was the first to speak, though her pride had been wounded by Lance's churlish behaviour at their first meeting.

"The wind has changed," she said. "Could not a vessel enter the port easily now, and lie safe at her moorings under the grand rocks? Is La Belle Marie gone?"

Lance came to the window, and looked at the waving boughs opposite. He did not answer her question.

"How came Mynheer to give you a passage?" he asked, suddenly. "He does not often choose to have strangers on board. Perhaps you have known him before?"

Reine's eyes filled with tears.

"Yes, and no!" she said. "He has known those who loved me. We cannot be strange to each other. In the sailing vessel which he commands, where all obey him at a word, and his will is law, he was like a father to me. I should be sorry," she added, after a pause, "if he were to be in trouble for bringing me to this place."

"No fear of that," said Lance. "La Belle Marie is a swift sailer. If the Curlew were rounding Arthur's Head, and the French schooner off Lezant Point, she would spread her wings like a bird, and be out of sight before the officer got his glass to bear upon her. He has more than one lesson to learn from experience before he catches Mynheer."

Reine worked on in silence for several minutes. Meanwhile, a large water-spaniel, which had come into the room with Lance, went up to her, as if to claim acquaintance. The animal was of a very staid demeanour, and looked as if he had been well cared for. His curly hair was crisp and clean, as well as remarkably fine. Reine bent over him lovingly.

"Bouffe recollects me," she said, after she had addressed a few French words to the dog, which he seemed to understand perfectly. "We were friends on board the schooner. Has Mynheer given him to you?"

"Yes. He brought him over for me from France. That was what took me to Lezant the other night. I expected the dog, and Jacob Mohr is a man of his word. These Bouffe dogs are rare, even in their own country, and can be trained to perform almost any feat by land or water. This one has been half worried already by the savage brutes in the yard; and though he showed fight, he did not bark. He has been taught to hunt his game silently."

Reine looked down compassionately at the handsome animal, now coiled up contentedly at her feet. "Ah, Bouffe, mon ami! we have both got to fight our way in the world. We must be allies."

She said no more; and Lance, who seldom spoke six words to a female, was equally silent.

"You were singing," he remarked, at last. "Why do you leave off? I do not

understand the words, but I like to hear you.
Besides, it must help you with your work."

"How is it that you do not speak French,
when your mother is married to a man who
is scarcely English? You must hear it often.
Those foreign vessels, too—you seem to have
dealings with their crews and captains. I
wonder you have not learned the language."

"I never liked a word I heard of it, before," said Lance. "But here and there I
catch your meaning. Those are the cries of
the hunters after the wolves, and some poor
mother has lost her child while the men of
the valley were on the mountains. There
now, you see, I have made out part of your
song. . Go on with it, I beg of you."

He walked away from the window, as he
spoke, and after a few minutes, during which
Reine remained silent, he left the room, but
he did not go far away. The girl, without
turning her head, could see him standing
under a clump of dark fir-trees near the
corner of the house. It was not possible for
Reine long to harbour an unkind thought.
She did not repeat the ballad he had asked
for; but, after a short interval, she began
singing a sea-song, which she had often heard
on board La Belle Marie.

It was one the sailors had brought with
them from their homes in Brittany, and the

sound of the sea-waves coming in upon the sandy beaches was imitated in the refrain. Then, the cry of the fishermen preparing their boats, amid plaintive partings from their wives and little ones. The boats are over the bar now—out on the wild waters, with the moon and stars dancing in bright reflections on the calm surface of the waters; and the men sing a hymn to the Virgin as they cast down their nets, praying for a full load ere morning.

Lance saw, when, upon Reine's suddenly stopping her song, he looked into the room, that his step-father had come in, and was sitting at the farther end, near the fireplace, where logs were laid—not lit, but ready for burning. The sun had gone round from that side of the house; and the corner, where Mr. Helier sat, was in deep shadow.

There was very little cordiality between the present occupant of Woods and his step-son. Some years before this time, Lance had broken the leading-strings in which his father-in-law tried to hold him. He was free now, and came and went as he liked. The Manor-house could hardly be called his abode, he spent so little of his time there, though he chose to maintain a claim to the rude chamber, which had been called his from his childhood, by occasionally occupying it. No person in

the house, except Mr. Fleming's old servant,
who had admitted Reine, dared to question
the youth about these frequent absences.

Bouffe heard the low, indistinct whistle,
like the call of a bird, with which Lance
turned off down one of the paths towards the
sea, and followed his master. Reine worked
on, struggling with a feeling of oppression,
for which she hardly knew how to account.
She felt more alone, with that dark-browed,
silent man for her companion, than she had
done while she was singing her pleasant
Breton songs in solitude.

Even when Mrs. Helier came in this sensation did not wear off. All his family were
afraid of the taciturn master of Woods; who,
though he had spent more than half his life
in England, had never been thoroughly na-
turalised. He was more of a foreigner in
manner, accent, and idiom, than his young
kinswoman, who had never visited this country before. Yet Reine, fond as she was of
sunny France, did not like him. He spoke
rarely, and took little heed of what passed;
but his temper, when roused, was very violent. At present, he sat with his head resting
on his hands, and his elbows on the table,
apparently tired, perhaps sleeping. His wife
moved about stealthily, not to disturb him.
Reine began to think Woods a very dull

place; but she worked on silently, as long as the daylight lasted.

Just as the room was beginning to grow really dark, a wild shriek rang through the passages of the old house. Mr. Helier looked up, his dark face pale with terròr; and a great white owl, disturbed from its nest in the ruins of the old chapel, flew close past the window, hooting, into the woods.

"Mon Dieu!" he exclaimed; "what sound is that? Are we never to be quiet? Quel tapage infernal! Will no one rid us of these horrors?"

"It is nothing," said Reine, cheerfully, after listening for a moment. "I hear laughing and talking;—the children are come in. Shall I go and see?"

Mr. Helier's face, at first pallid, grew red with anger, as childish voices and laughter sounded nearer.

"Ah, ce n'est rien que les enfans!" he said, with concentrated fury. "I will teach them how to play at that! Restez ici. Let no one stir till I come back. This all must finish."

He went out hurriedly. Reine's heart quailed when she heard real sobs and shrieks of pain in the passage. Presently, Mr. Helier, not looking like the same man, his countenance full of furious excitement, came in, dragging his eldest daughter by the wrist, which was red with the pressure of his hard fingers.

"Let me see," he said, "which of you is it that I am to punish? Will you play the revenant again at Woods? Was it Lance who set you on?"

"No, no!" said both the terrified girls, in a breath. "Lance is angry if we talk about the ghost. He does not play with us. Oh, father, please to let us go, and we will never do it again!"

"Oh, you confess! you are the troublers of this house," said the irritated father, raising his arm with such violent anger that Reine hastily came to the rescue. As she moved forward, the red marks on the girl's wrist, which she was struggling to release, caught the man's notice. He seemed half frightened at his own rising passion, and made an effort to subdue it.

"There, there! that will do. Mademoiselle is kind enough to speak for you. Zélie! Victoire! Let me hear no more of these horrible noises. I thought we should have been quiet for a while. The house has been more tranquil lately."

He laid his head down again upon his clasped hands, and slept or dozed till supper was brought in; but he complained of indisposition, and touched nothing. The girls, wild, uncouth creatures, chattered together in a corner, or pulled about Reine's work, tearing the net, entangling the fine cotton, and making destructive havoc with their long, listless fingers, which were never quiet.

Meanwhile, the wind rose, and sang round the building with its thousand wild voices, as it rustled among the branches, moaned in the chimneys, or echoed loudly, each time a distant door opened, along the passages. Sometimes, one of the boughs of the tall elm-trees nearest to the house swept across the window from which Reine had retreated, and scuds of rain rattled against the casement panes. It was a dark, dreary night; and within, the frightened children, their habitually pale, timid mother, and the silent man, with his face buried in his hands, were not more cheerful than the ravings of the storm.

Lance Fleming's dog — the smuggling Captain's present — crept after Reine to her chamber, and she did not like to drive it away. In the middle of the night she awoke, with a strong sensation of terror. It was only Bouffe, pulling at the cloak she had thrown over the scantily-furnished couch. At the same time, there was a dull sound of shuffling feet in the long gallery:

For a moment, Reine thought of the reports she had heard of supernatural visitations there; but the dog's instinct might be trusted, and Bouffe seemed to know that friends rather than enemies were outside. A long, low, most unghostlike whistle settled the question, and the girl got up, and putting the cloak round her, crossed the floor, and opened the door just wide enough to let out her dumb companion.

She was sure that it was Lance who had summoned the dog, and she fancied that he said, "Thank you," and "Good night," in a more civilised manner than might have been expected. The night was fine, now, though not clear; and, as she looked from her window over the woodland scenery, she could see a star or two shining through the mist. Nothing else was visible: the trees deepened and darkened into a shadowy, indistinct mass; and she was uncertain whether what she heard was the faint, sighing sound of the wind among the branches, or the distant murmur of the sea. While she was trying to ascertain this point, a bright light shot up high in the west, and fell in a shower of sparks, like shooting stars, across the dark grey sky.

Reine had watched the sailors of La Belle Marie sending rockets aloft, as they declared, for her amusement; but, as she guessed, to serve as signals to the smugglers along the coast. Her heart beat as she remembered words spoken unguardedly in her hearing when on board; and, while the sparks went out slowly, one after another, she longed to know whether this was the concerted warning that the Curlew, one of the smartest Revenue cutters in the service, with her dashing young Commander, Lieutenant Osborne, was on the watch off the entrance of the harbour of Lezant.

CHAPTER III.

LEZANT Church was unusually crowded the next morning. That Sunday was the first since the power of the Church, and the prayers of its Minister, had been called upon to quiet the nocturnal disturbances at Woods; and Mr. St. Erme's congregation wanted to see how their old Parson looked after his conflict with the ghost.

He was still in appearance the model of a reverend divine — tall, slender, silver-haired — with a voice like the sighing of the autumn wind, as it came softened through the Parsonage evergreens, after lifting up its shrill clarion-call upon the cliffs. When he now rose up to address his more than ordinarily attentive flock, some degree of pity was felt for him. His bent form, white, trembling hands, and feeble accents, showed that a change for the worse had been wrought in him; but Mr. St. Erme was not a man likely to reveal in his sermon the tenor of the thoughts which had occupied him, or the events which might have diversified his existence during the past week. The cool stream of his oratory flowed on unaltered, rising and falling with just its old cadences. For anything he told them, Life might have been as unreal as the metaphors and similes with which he decked it.

It was said by the older inhabitants of Lezant, that, when he first came among them, Mr. St. Erme, though rather far-fetched and obscure in his language, had been a somewhat eloquent preacher. His own inner life was that of a man possessed by strong though mystical religious feelings; but, whatever energies he had once possessed, were now dead within him. He had no sympathy with his flock: early education and habits had placed him too much above them; and pride, wounded in its tenderest point, made him shrink from contact with those who were acquainted with the nature of the sore hidden and rankling under that cold, dignified exterior.

For nearly thirty years the incumbent of this secluded parish, Reginald St. Erme, had so contrived to exist that he was, if possible, more ignorant of the spiritual requirements of its inhabitants, than when, fresh from college triumphs, he was first inducted to the living on the presentation of its patron, Lord Boscawen. He had then crossed the Bodmin Moors with some dismay; and he still looked back upon the distant wavy heights which shut him out from the civilised world, with the feelings of a man who has endured a long and painful exile.

Though he had spent more than half his life among them, he yet felt himself a stranger to the persons he encountered, whenever, as was but rarely the case, he walked along the busy thoroughfare of Lezant. In his own church he was more at home; and, Sunday after Sunday he ascended the pulpit, and preached to those brawny mariners and fishermen sermons which would have been more appropriate to some collegiate chapel.

No matter that, but a short half mile from the church, lay that great, vasty deep, to which so many of them went down in ships and came back no more!—that, on many a Sabbath, his harmonious but not forcible organ of speech was overpowered by the eddying wind and volleying thunder, and the hoarse roar of the waves, as the drift of the Atlantic set in against those iron-ribbed cliffs, beneath which so many a gallant vessel, with its precious human freight, had gone to pieces. The ocean-billows, the wind, the thunder—even the minute-guns at sea—might, with their own terrible innate signification, solemnise his discourse; but no lesson was drawn from them by the preacher. He was there, in the round

of accustomed duty, to perform for a certain
number of hours and minutes the services of
the Church, and deal forth some admonitory
precepts to the people; and if wrecks on the
shore — as had been the case within the memory of man — had left every bench empty,
he would have finished his exhortation.

The church stood outside the village, on
very high ground, facing the sea, which had
washed deep caverns in the cliff. All around,
tossed up and down, lay the undulating surface of the Cornish moor; excepting where,
in a deeper, combe-like dip of the hill, screened
by thick plantations and shrubberies, but still
commanding a fine view of the sea and cliffs,
the Rectory-house and gardens retreated from
sight.

A happy life might have been spent under
the roof of Lezant Parsonage; but Mr. St.
Erme's destiny was a perverse one. Disappointed at an early age in what might have
softened a naturally peculiar disposition, he
had never married; and the hopes he had
afterwards garnered up, and by which he had
set more store than should attach to any
earthly treasure or anticipation, had been
scattered, like the frail hawthorn and labur-
num blossoms that streamed over the moors
from the outside of his parterres, when the
wild sea-blasts whirled them away.

Often now, as the Rector paced slowly, with failing step and downcast eyes, up and down that gravel walk which formed, winter and summer, almost his only place for taking exercise, he would hear, close behind or beside him, a quicker, manlier footfall, not unlike his own in the tread, but more firmly planted. A voice which reminded him of home — of that magic circle of affections which, once broken, had never for him been re-created — would speak words put together and pronounced as only one person on earth had ever uttered them. On those green cliffs, as he well remembered, that handsome, stately form, so often present to his thoughts, might have been seen whiling away the hours which sometimes hung heavily at Lezant Rectory. Never did the bells of distant churches ring over that wide expanse, without recalling the memory of the day when he had watched anxiously every member of his wayward flock appear and take his accustomed seat, without seeing his brother enter the house of prayer.

At either end of a table covered with snowy damask and old-fashioned French china, in the sunny morning-room at Lezant Parsonage, — eighteen years before the Sunday when Mr. St. Erme has been described preaching to his turbulent parishioners, — the Rector and his brother were seated at breakfast. Both were tall, handsome men, in the prime of life; but the country clergyman and magistrate, though, in fact, the younger of the two, looked older than the man of camps and courts. Colonel St. Erme had seen some hard service abroad, and now held an appointment in the royal household. He had married early, and been left a widower. A very strong affection, by no means ostenta-tiously brought forward, existed between the brothers; they were alike fastidious, refined, and haughty. Often, in public life, the cour-tier and soldier met with jars and disappoint-ments, which were confided only to his recluse brother.

At such times the Cornish hermitage, as he called it, smiled a pleasant welcome to him; while to the quieter, but scarcely more satisfied spirit of the dweller in the wastes, these occasional visits appeared as bright .spots marked strongly in the dull calendar of the year's events.

Ever and anon the Rector glanced at his sermon, which lay in its neat case on the breakfast-table beside him; but still he lin-gered, listening to anecdotes not much in character with the text he had chosen for the heading of his grave discourse. At another moment he might have heard without pain his brother's careless expressions; but, with the holy calm of the Sabbath morning round him, and the words of solemn preparation for prayer almost on his lips, he longed to choose some graver subject of conversation. The fear, however, of giving offence, and putting an end to the pleasant habit of frank, unrestrained confidence, which they had maintained from boyhood, for some time kept him silent.

He was relieved when Colonel St. Erme, rising from table, went to the window, and stood admiring the landscape, as he always did, winter or summer, when he came to Lezant. There was, indeed, no season when those verdant grounds, with the undulating downs beyond, and brightly sparkling ocean, were not beautiful; but the Rector, who was not so ardent a lover of nature as his brother, never enjoyed the place so much as when he saw how greatly it ministered to the gratification of his favourite guest.

He was a fine classical scholar, and longed to tread the shores of Greece and Italy; but there were no associations which interested him, connected with the Cornish tors, and the broad sweeps of the hills, heaved up in masses, on which the light fell, broken by the cloud shadows.

The travelled man of the world, conscious that his present tranquil existence was but a thing of the moment, which he could change as soon as it palled upon him, professed himself never weary of gazing upon that glorious prospect.

"Upon my word, Reginald, I envy you! Lezant is the pleasantest place I know," he ended with observing. "You must excuse me if I am a defaulter from church this sunshiny afternoon. There is something positively irresistible in the aspect of those cliffs."

"Do not stay away without a better reason, Edmund," said his brother, affectionately. "Our one weekly service is not too severe a task upon your powers of attention. You will have plenty of time for a stroll on the cliffs before it begins; or I will go with you afterwards. It gives me pain to see the ordinances of the Church neglected, especially by one staying under my roof; and I am sorry to say mine is but a scanty congregation. Besides, I have prepared my sermon with much care; and I should like to have one intelligent listener. I think it will interest you."

"I am sorry that I cannot hear it this afternoon. You must preach it over again some other Sunday for me. The fact is, Reginald," he said, seeing that his brother looked mortified, "Fleming and I have had a

quarrel. He does me the honour to be jealous, and swears I shall not speak to his
pretty wife. Now, I am not going to be
dictated to by him; and, at the same time, I
should not wish to be a party to a brawl at
your church-door: so the only plan I can
adopt is to keep away. He is hardly enough
of the gentleman for me to call him out; but
if he ill-uses Mrs. Fleming, as he has done
once or twice in my presence, I shall certainly
be constrained to teach him better manners."

"Do not interfere between them, Edmund!" said his brother, anxiously. "The
Flemings are a most unhappy couple. You
cannot mend, but may make matters worse.
Though he is distantly related to Lord Boscawen, Fleming is fast losing every pretension
to be regarded as a gentleman. His habits are
low and intemperate. What pleasure can a person like yourself derive from such society?"

"You are quite right, Reginald. Fleming
is a brute!" Colonel St. Erme answered, with
strong indignation. "How shamefully he
treats his poor wife! There was a red mark
yesterday on her wrist, which is not larger
than my Mary's. I should not like to know
how she came by it."

"She is a weak, vain coquette. I wonder
you name her in the same breath with your
little daughter!" said the Rector, gravely.'

" Fleming's temper, especially when aggravated, as it constantly is by intoxication, is quite ungovernable. He will illtreat his wife more and more, and probably insult you, if you offer her attentions, which are considered in quite another light in this parish from that in which they probably appear to a man of your gay habits. These people of Lezant are no triflers, but a dogged, hardened race, ready to impute to you a worse design than the mere foolish flirtation into which her light speech and conduct have led you. Connected with this heartless amusement are a thousand disagreeable contingencies for me, for you, and, above all, for this poor, silly woman. Give it up, I entreat you!"

Colonel St. Erme coloured. " You would not have me own myself in the wrong, by withdrawing attentions which are no more than any pretty woman might claim as her due? Let us say no more on the subject."

The Rector took up his sermon, and retreated to his study, while his brother left the house and sauntered towards the cliffs, where he often lay basking for hours in the sunshine. When he reached the summit of the grassy promontory which overlooked the town and the surrounding country, he threw himself down on the turf, and remained for some time idly watching the different groups wending their way to church, from farm-houses hidden in nooks among the downs; masters and mistresses, with their labourers and domestics, the women riding, according to the universal fashion in Cornwall, and merry children running on in front.

When the latest laggard of the congregation had entered the portal of the sacred edifice, Colonel St. Erme rose and walked for some distance along the edge of the cliff, in the direction of the Manor Farm. He had not gone far, when, along the road he had been watching, which wound with a tortuous course through the valley, came the pretty mistress of Woods, mounted on her favourite horse, the best in her husband's stables. She blushed when he accosted her, and said that she was returning home by the short bridle-path over the cliffs, on account of having left her little boy ailing. Mr. Fleming had said she ought to go to church; but, when she got half way, she felt so anxious about Lance, that she had persuaded him to let her go back. Whatever might have been her previous intentions, her pace was slow, as she rode with Colonel St. Erme's hand upon the rein of her horse, guiding him past the dangerous gaps in the cliff to the gates of Woods, where she took leave of him.

Colonel St. Erme returned to the Parson-

age in time to dress for dinner. He did not
mention to his brother any intention he had
formed of leaving Lezant, but seemed to be
in good spirits, admiring, with his usual zest,
the moonlight view, which was even more
beautiful than the brilliant morning sunshine
had been. Whenever the Colonel was staying
with his brother, he lost no opportunity
of going out to enjoy such a spectacle;
and now, the moon being at the full, he
possessed himself of the Rector's private key,
and went through the grounds to the summit
of the promontory. The light lay in golden
masses on the sea, while against the rocks,
which stood out blacker than ever by contrast, the tide rolled in thunderingly, filling
the curious caverns and inlets with which the
coast was indented. The broad surface of
the hills, heaved up in wild ridges and hollows, gleamed white through mist; and the
dark wooded chasm, in which the waterfalls
kept up a continual chant, brooded in unbroken darkness.

At a late hour of that bright summer
night, Mrs. Fleming was sitting up nursing
her little boy in a room called, from its furniture, the Walnut-wood Chamber, at the
old manor-house in the ravine. There was
a fire burning, for the place was damp at all
seasons, and the white moonbeams fell

through the wide window upon the floor, almost meeting the red reflection from the hearth. She had gone to bed early, but had risen when the child cried, and thrown upon the iron dogs occupying the place of a modern grate a large oak bough, which was sparkling and crackling half way up the spacious chimney. The young woman cowered over the fire, crying silently; for the last words which had passed between Fleming and herself had been angry ones, and she had been forced to bear even harsher tokens of his displeasure. He had gone out late, and would probably return mad with drink; — she knew not that her life was safe in that lone place, now that jealousy had kindled his worst passions.

Very different words dwelt in her recollection—kind, soothing, almost tender compliments—flattering glances which had lately been almost too familiar. Very bitterly she contrasted those courtly adulations with her husband's savage violence; and yet henceforward, Fleming had told her, in terms which she knew were no idle threats, that she was not to hold speech with the Colonel. She would be running a very terrible risk if she again disobeyed him.

As the night wore on, she took stealthily from a drawer in an old cabinet a very hand-

some hunting-watch in a chased gold cover,
and, pressing the spring, made it repeat the
hour. She was dreadfully troubled in mind
about the safest mode of returning this costly
trinket to its owner. Colonel St. Erme had
lent it to her a few days previously, bidding
her, jestingly, keep better time at church;
and hinting plainly that he should waylay her
in her homeward route, in case she preferred,
like himself, to watch the influx of the highest
tide of the year, instead of listening to the
Rector's sermon.

In her hurry to get ready, when Fleming
called her to accompany him, she had left
the watch behind her; and now she trembled
at the idea of mentioning that she had it in
her possession. Hour after hour went by,
and at last she began to wonder that Fleming
did not come home. She looked from the
window, but all the woods were hushed; not
an owl, nor a nighthawk, disturbed their
stillness. White waves of moonlight—deep
masses of shade—lay stretched out before
her. Then the child, when it heard her
moving, cried out, and the necessary task of
soothing it occupied her. Again the boy
dropped off to sleep; but now a vaguer,
wilder fear, kept the mother watching.
Though unkindness had grown up between
her and her husband, who had taught her to

dread him in his angry moods, and had now
left home in company she disliked, Phœbe
Fleming would have given the world to hear
his returning footstep; but though she waited
up till daylight, he came not.

The next morning it was the same.
Search was made, and on the unfrequented
beach, over which, on the previous afternoon,
the great flood-tide of the year had swept,
the body of the unfortunate tenant of the
Grange was found by his servants. It was
supposed, at first, that he had met with an
accident, while returning home intoxicated
from the village. He had been seen to take
the path leading over Lezant headland, just
at the time when, as it was afterwards proved,
Colonel St. Erme let himself out upon the
cliff from the Parsonage garden.

The sentence which followed the verdict
of the Cornish jury would undoubtedly have
been carried into effect, and the utmost
penalty of the law endured by the convicted
murderer, had not a cooler and more dispas-
sionate judgment been formed elsewhere of a
case resting so entirely upon circumstantial
evidence. Mitigated, as it was, by the mercy
of the Crown, Colonel St. Erme's doom
amounted to utter ruin and perpetual disgrace. It was with difficulty that he was
prevailed upon to admit even his brother to a

parting interview; and, when this painful leave-taking was over, his chief desire became to depart immediately for his allotted place of exile. Degraded as he was to the rank of a criminal, he considered the greatest benefit which could accrue to his children and friends would be that his existence should be absolutely forgotten. If he had maintained during his banishment any communication with his family, it was kept profoundly secret.

Mr. St. Erme had never recovered from the shock of his brother's trial and condemnation. He retired at once from society, and buried himself completely in the profound repose of the Cornish Rectory. It would have been better for him if this retreat, obscure as he had always considered it, had been farther removed from the scene of the dreadful catastrophe which blighted his life; but he had not energy enough left even to attempt to negotiate an exchange of livings. When, through the interest of friends, a very advantageous proposal to that effect was made to him, he declined it.

His morbid feelings made him shrink alike from new faces and from those to which he was accustomed. Neither sympathy nor compassion was agreeable to him. Even in the fulfilment of the duties which devolved upon him, he found no comfort. He had un-

dertaken the care of his unfortunate brother's
children, but when they were brought to him
he could not bear to look upon them. The
confiscation of Colonel St. Erme's property
had, of course, greatly altered their prospects;
shame and disgrace must for the future attend their lot in life; mortifications beset
whatever path they might follow. In pur-
suance of these gloomy ideas, the boy was
sent abroad to receive his education at a
school in Brittany, while the girl dwelt in
unbroken seclusion beneath her uncle's roof.

His own disposition became every year
more harsh and misanthropical. For ever
dwelling on one intensely painful subject, his
mind narrowed as he contemplated it. An
austerity foreign in youth to his character
grew upon him. Nothing that was new or
entertaining found its way through his closed
doors. Year after year he revolved over and
over again the same thoughts, read the same
books, performed the same circumscribed
round of duties, and administered the same
formal charities. The overflowing kindnesses
which endear a pastor to his flock, the daily
offices of love, were not expected from the
Rector of Lezant. Nothing would have surprised his parishioners more than to discover
that this silent, abstracted mortal, had so many
turbulent human emotions stirring within

him. He was regarded as a cold, eccentric scholar, divided from them by learning, by anchoritish habits, and by a morose, unsympathetic humour.

The only link of connexion between the Rector and his flock was the pale, fair girl, who walked close beside him, on the Sunday in question, past the latest lingerers in the churchyard. Mary St. Erme had lived from her earliest childhood at Lezant Parsonage. Deprived by death of a mother's love in infancy, and by a yet more cruel fate of a father's care—separated from her only brother—there was nothing to make the young girl's heart and mind expand in the chill atmosphere of her uncle's dwelling. To him she was but a painful memento of past sufferings. He sometimes fancied the retrospect would have been less bitter, if her pale face did not constantly remind him of the blight which had swept over all connected with his unhappy brother.

Though he had never confided to her his depth of grief, Mary St. Erme guessed the trouble that lay hidden under that cold exterior. In spite of the want of love from which she had suffered, her own sympathies were large and overflowing. The rude but not heartless people of Lezant said that she knew everybody's sorrows, and her presence brought balm to many an aching heart.

Not that her own mind was at ease. A very perturbed spirit looked out upon the world from those deep-set eyes. As she walked by her uncle's side, Sunday after Sunday, or listened to the dreamy flow of his eloquence, a deep compassion for the wants of the congregation to whom he was so ill-suited awoke within her. Even while she was spoken of affectionately as one upon whom the hand of the Almighty had been laid afflictingly, and who was visited with that kind of mental deficiency which, among the poor, is regarded with reverence, Mary St. Erme was reading their hearts. Debarred from other learning, she studied the Scriptures, deriving from them lessons which were tested by accurate personal observation. Gliding among them at all hours — surrounded by a purity and holiness which arose from her extreme simplicity — she was as an angel of light to the villagers, counteracting the ill-effect which her uncle's faulty discharge of his sacred duties would otherwise have had upon them, and throwing over his declining years the veil which charity and mercy like hers alone can spread.

From time immemorial there had been no second service in the church; and Mr. St. Erme was not a person to institute changes. No one saw any more of him when, his light Sunday duty performed, the gate of the Rec-

tory garden closed behind him, and the evergreens hid him from view. As soon as the
congregation dispersed the public-houses in the
village were filled ; except when, as on the present occasion, a crowd collected round one of
the numerous Methodist preachers, whom a
sudden revival from a state of almost hea-
thenish apathy had sent forth at that period
into the most distant corners of the land. At
the top of the main street, just opposite to
the Three Crowns, a Ranter was vehemently
holding forth. There was more substance in
what he told them, the sailors said, than in
the Parson's wishy-washy sermon.

"We shall have him turning Methody
next. Just look at the old fellow!" said the
lame soldier, contemptuously, pointing out
the fine, saint-like head of his father, Simon
Brock, as he sat by the small window of the
Three Crowns, listening to the preacher. "I
say, mother! if you let this go on, he'll be
for making the house into a Meeting. I'll
not stop, for one, if there's anything of that
sort brewing. You'll have your license taken
away, and lose the best of our customers.
You know what a row there was about the
new hymn-books—Methody psalms, people
called them. The Three Crowns is the ortho-
dox inn of the place, and I won't have new
fashions set up. Let the Boscawen Arms

preach and pray! We are a loyal public—
witness our sign—and hold by the Crown,
the Bishops, and the Corporation!"

"Hold your tongue, Andrew!" said his
mother. "What harm does the old man's
nonsense do you? I wish you were half as
quiet. He's praying in his heart now, poor
fellow! and I'm not going to hinder him.
It isn't to church you've been yourself this
morning, you godless, irreverent sinner!
though you've not lifted a hand to work.
Just listen to what the man's saying. He's
got a word of power, anyhow. Hark how
he's hurling it out, right and left, against the
rich people!"

The dame went to the door, and stood
complacently listening to the preacher's de-
nunciations of a burning judgment against
the great men of the earth; but when,
changing his subject, he inveighed against
drunkenness, she came quickly inside the
house.

"Let be!" she said. "He's going beyond his depth now. Folks must live; and it's
neither Law nor Gospel to say they're not to
eat and drink. Where would be the use of
keeping a public if that was forbidden? I
won't have anybody in my house listen to
such trash. I say, old man, haven't you had
enough of it?"

"Yes, yes; shut the window. It's not what Miss Mary reads to me," said the old man. "There was a word or two at first, but he's gone astray from his text, and talks nothing but foolishness. I wonder, will she come to me to-day? I wish I could read a bit for myself."

He turned over, disconsolately, the leaves of the Bible, which, in his ignorance, was a sealed book to him. Meanwhile, the preacher, finding that his audience was thinning, moved away, followed by some of the idle stragglers of the place.

"He's going to hold out before the Boscawen Arms — bless him! — I'll be bound for it," said Mrs. Brock, grimly. "Much good may it do them! It's dry work listening; and perhaps, let him say what he will, people may drop in and take a glass. Well, I don't grudge it them. Poor creatures, it's little business they're like to get! Not enough to cover their outlay."

While Dame Brock was bustling about, making preparations for the receipt of the custom which, later in the day, was sure to flock to the place, there came past the crowded corner, where the preacher was again holding forth, a light, girlish form. Mary St. Erme had gone fearlessly among the rough smuggling population of Lezant from her childhood. In her

bearing there was a mixture of simplicity,
purity, and refinement, which, while it raised
her above, did not separate her from them.
While fevers had crept from house to house
along the street, decimating the occupants of
the ill-ventilated dwellings, she had not feared
to visit them. Her calm, holy aspect rebuked
vice, and the boldest sinner doffed his cap,
and blessed her as she passed. There was no
swearing, or even loud speaking, among the
stragglers on the outskirts of the crowd, who
had been mocking at the enthusiast's fervour,
till she was out of hearing.

The hostess of the Three Crowns curtseyed to the young lady, who, passing by her
silently, went to the farther end of the long
room, where the old man, at this hour of the
Sabbath, usually looked for her coming. His
infirmities prevented his attending church,
but he dearly loved to have the Bible read to
him. No one ever intruded upon her when
Mary St. Erme was thus engaged, though the
men of the village would sometimes gather
round the open door and listen. It was the
only time when, as Simon Brock often said,
his own house seemed to belong to him.

There was no loud talking or jesting
among those in the outer room of the inn
now. The men, rough as they were, held
their breaths as the delicate girl came among

them. The church in the morning, especially towards the close of Mr. St. Erme's long sermon, had not been half so quiet. There was something in the expression of those spiritual eyes—in the light that sat throned on that fair brow, which made the rudest brawler hold his peace. One or two of the more respectable of Dame Brock's customers shrank out of sight, as if ashamed to be caught in that place on the Lord's Day; but no one actually left the house. Miss St. Erme, however, looked at no one; she seemed only conscious of the presence of the old man, to whom she spoke kindly, in a low tone, and then took up the sacred volume to read to him.

Not a single rude sound disturbed her. Dame Brock folded her hands demurely in her apron, and sat down, after giving a sound cuff to her son, to prevent his rattling his crutch upon the floor. The Three Crowns seldom was so orderly.

Whether or not she was in reality conscious that others besides old Simon Brock were listening, and that half the men about the door were sailors, Mary's selection of a chapter pleased her auditors. The perils of the storm—to many of them a familiar theme—when, firm in faith, Paul, a bound prisoner, encouraged the sailors to stand by the ship—the

loss of all save life — the kindness of the bar-
barous islanders — interested the seamen. Her
clear, sweet voice seemed to fill the room as
the young girl read on, her own interest en-
thralled in the narrative, and feeling as only
those can feel who, living by the sea, look
daily on its solemn face, and have committed
what they love most on earth to its keeping.

" ' Except these abide in the ship ye cannot be saved,' " said the old man, dreamily,
when at last she paused. " Were not those
Paul's words? I shall be saying them all the
day after you leave me. There are no such
words spoken here when you're gone, and I
can't find them for myself. Folks sit out
yonder, and say things that can't be right.
I 'd as lieve not hear them."

" That 's good reading," the dame remarked, when Miss St. Erme closed the book.
" His Reverence preached a fine discourse
this morning, I 'm told. I wish it may do
them good that had the privilege of listening.
It isn't often I 'm able to get so far; but I 'm
not like some folk that attend his worship's
church by day, and then at night go to the
Meeting. I never had any opinion of con-
venticles and barn-preachers. If we don't
stand by the Establishment it 's not to be expected that the gentry should support us.
The old man is a deal quieter always when

the young lady has been reading to him. I
wish he heard it oftener."

"It's the only thing in life I care for,
now," said the old man; "and there's but
one voice says the words rightly. I've not
heard the Bible read in church since I got
crippled like—tied to my own chimney-
corner, where I'm forced to see many things
go on that's contrary to the teaching of that
book. No, nor it doesn't please me to listen
to texts and citing of the Holy Scriptures,
from lips that are, maybe, chaffing and
swearing at other times."

Dame Brock glanced at him with subdued
fury.

"Hark to his ungratefulness!" she said.
"Because I'm forced to look to the business
that he's not been able to mind these eighteen
years, and can't read like his Reverence and
the young lady, I'm to be told the Blessed
Book is not fit for the likes of me! But I'm
prepared for it. We must bear what is put
upon us, only doing our duty by the gentry
and the public, and see what comes of it.
Andrew, lad!" she exclaimed, sharply, "art
turned to stone? Look out, and tell us
what's going on down street; it's not so quiet
as it was. What's in the wind, now, I
wonder?"

The dame, unable to control her impatience, stepped forth into the midst of the crowd which had gathered in the porch.

"What is it, my masters?" she asked, seeing their excitement. "Is there news forward? This wind was sure to bring vessels into port. Well, day or night we're ready to receive them. There's always some one about and stirring at the Three Crowns. We don't shut the shutters and bar the doors at nine o'clock, like the Boscawen Arms people. All are welcome to enter."

"Yes, if they choose to come," said Andrew, sullenly. "There's word passed up street the Boscawen has got a regular housewarming. Every room's chock full."

Dame Brock's face turned crimson. "I'll not believe it," she said. "Come in, you fool! What do you stand staring there for? Customers don't drop from the clouds. Come in, I say. We've as many as we can serve already." She curtseyed to Miss St. Erme, who had risen, and was taking leave of the old man. "Wouldn't the young lady condescend to read us another chapter? I declare it was quite edifying to see how they were all listening. I don't know what's set them wild. There's nothing like Scripture readings to make people quiet."

The lame soldier took his mother by the

arm, and drew her out upon the nap, whence a portion of the harbour was visible. "Look out there," he said, pointing with his finger; "yonder, between the houses."

For once in her life Dame Brock's fluency was checked, as her quick eye followed the indication. Her usually ruddy complexion grew a shade paler when she perceived a vessel standing in, with the King's colours flying. The men were all watching her.

While they stood silent, with some degree of consternation imprinted on every countenance, Miss St. Erme glided through the group at the inn door, stopping, as she passed, for one single moment, to ask an old mariner a question. She did not pause again till she was on the high ground above every house in the town, which commanded a view of the open sea, and of the narrow entrance commonly called the Devil's Grip. A boat was putting off from the newly-arrived vessel, and she waited till the rowers threw up their oars at the steps just below the new inn. Over her fair young face, which bore the marks of deep trouble, there passed a grievous expression of anxiety, and she lingered irresolutely after she had raised the latch of a gate opening into the churchyard, through which there was a path to the Rectory garden. Mary

St. Erme did not pass through, but walked
up and down the crowded resting-place of the
dead, with her blue, thoughtful eyes sadly
fixed on the emblems of mortality, the low
headstones deep sunk in grass on all sides of
her.

CHAPTER IV.

WHILE, for once in a way, the usually rude
and noisy inn kept by Dame Brock was
hushed into Sabbath stillness, the much more
orderly and respectable house of entertainment by the waterside was a scene of bustling
confusion.   Mary St. Erme's auditors would
hardly have listened so quietly, had it been
made known to them earlier that, between
the black precipitous walls of jagged rock,
which sank so sheer down into the water, that
a vessel of three hundred tons burthen could
thread that narrow strait, and ride safe at
anchor in the inlet,—a Government cutter,
with her tall straight mast visible at intervals
over the rounded tops of the steep bluffs,
was gliding swiftly into Lezant harbour.
The young officer in command of the
Curlew watched her progress with anxiety,
causing frequent soundings to be taken, and
carefully noting a small chart of the coast, to
which he was a stranger; but the lead sank
deep into the clear dark water; and, though

it seemed as if those on board the vessel
might almost have touched the steep crags on
either hand, the information he had received
before leaving the Welsh port where he had
touched last turned out to be correct.   Wind
and tide favouring, the passage, though re-
quiring caution, was perfectly practicable.

A crowd speedily collected on the quay,
while the Revenue cutter rounded the points
of the inlet, and, finally, as if satisfied with
her new quarters, anchored in the narrow
roadstead.

On this occasion the water-side inn was
destined to find favour in the eyes of the strangers ; and the young couple lately established
there, whose feelings had been bitterly mortified
by the neglect displayed for the attractions of
their new sign and superior accommodation,
were gratified by seeing the officer just landed
from the cutter, direct his steps at once to the
open door of the Boscawen Arms.   Having
ordered that refreshments should be supplied to
him, and looked with apparent satisfaction into
the small, neat parlour, freshly papered and car-
peted, to which one of the sailors had already
carried a writing case and valise, the young man
came out into the half-finished porch, and
stood, with his cap pulled low over his brows,
to screen his eyes from the glaring sunshine,
gazing with much curiosity at the singular

features of the scenery, as if they were absolutely new to him.

He was not left to the enjoyment of solitary meditation for more than a few moments,
of which, judging by the attentiveness of his
survey, he probably made good use. Customers were not plentiful at the new inn,
which had been set up on speculation by a
person who was not a native of the place.
Lieutenant Osborne had scarcely had time to
note down in his mental tablets the peculiar
formation of the rocky inlet, the promise of
shelter afforded by the little harbour, and the
contingencies which must render it at times
unapproachable, when a frank-looking, sailor-
like man came from the door of the tap-room,
which was quite separate from the dwelling-
house, and joined him, touching his cap as respectfully as if he had been one of his own crew.

For some time the two seamen, for they
had both been brought up to the same profession, talked only of the nature of the harbour, and the shortness of the period taken
by the cutter to make her passage from
Swansea. The Lieutenant was evidently proud
of his vessel, and it was not the landlord's
interest to decry the goodly craft which had
brought custom to his door. The Curlew
having received her full meed of praise, the
Lieutenant turned his attention inland.

"That is a good name," he said, looking at the sign swinging over the road. "I hope it brings you custom. Do any of the Boscawen family reside in the place?"

The young sailor hesitated; too frank to utter a falsehood, yet unwilling to confess how little benefit had been derived, hitherto, from the patronage he had respectfully solicited and been graciously promised by his lordship's steward.

Not exactly, he said, in answer to the officer's question. There were rumours that the old place belonging to the Boscawens might change hands. It was greatly to be desired that the family should reside. Were that to be the case, they would certainly patronise the only reputable inn at Lezant. Until now, the accommodation for travellers had been so bad, that the natural advantages of the place were thrown away. Not one tourist in a hundred turned off to visit them. But times were mending. The port had been improved, and the present road to the quay completed. Great expense had been incurred, but he and others had every reason to hope for a good return for their outlay.

The Lieutenant listened good-humouredly to the young publican's account of his not very flourishing prospects, which ended with his saying that, when trade was slack in the winter, he could always have a berth on board one of his uncle's vessels. He had a coal-yard at Swansea, and his boats often put in at Lezant. It had been a help to his nephew to get supplied with cheaper goods by water than he could purchase, after the expense of land-carriage to this remote spot.

"I am sure you are too honest a fellow to get your goods, as I understand other persons in your way of business do, at Lezant," said the officer, quickly. "I am to watch all comers and goers; and, remember, I do not do things by halves. If you serve the Crown honestly, I think you will find it a better trade than your opponents. The coast will be more closely watched than it has been."

"With all my heart, sir," the man answered, looking at him cheerfully. "I have been a sailor all my life, and though not in a King's ship, more 's the pity, I believe I know my duty to my country better than to deceive the Government we live under. It sickens me to see the tricks the people here play to get things free of charge to the revenue, and spending what they gain in drunkenness and profanity. Why, if the place was kept as it ought to be, what would hinder my lord's steward holding a court at Lezant, instead of at Camelford, when the rents are paid half-yearly? but there were such rows among the townspeople and tenantry, that no gentleman would put up with the nuisance. Perhaps we may all live to see it altered, and then there's no doubt the Boscawen Arms would be the place. My lord's steward as good as promised it."

He turned off to some of his various duties in the house, leaving his wife, a young, handsome woman, with two pretty children clinging to her skirts, to answer the stranger's questions.

"I am afraid he is too sanguine," she said, looking after him. "I almost wish we had set up among our own friends at Swansea. Lezant is a strange, wild place. Please God, we'll do better soon. I should not mind, if there was not so much malice in their hearts against us."

Her eyes filled with tears, and the young officer said kindly,—

"Have you no friends in the place? I do not see a single respectable habitation but your own; still, I suppose there must be others. Is the village hidden by that great headland?"

"Yes, sir. There are houses, plenty of them, but not of a sort that I like," she answered. "There are no respectable families in Lezant, such as you might expect from the size of the place; only poor fishing people—smugglers, one and all."

"But you must have a clergyman," said the Lieutenant, looking at his watch. "Is there any service, afternoon or evening, that I could attend? I always like to go to church when I am on shore, and I saw the tower peeping over the brow of the promontory. I almost fancied I could hear the bells."

"No; we have no bells here. I miss them so! But ours is a silent tower," said the woman, mournfully. "It is a fine old building, and we have service; once only, however. You're too late for it now, sir. There is a story that our bells were lost when they were just fresh cast, and sent down by Lord Boscawen from London. Some say, they sound in a storm from the water's depths now, but not in such weather as this. You could not have heard anything like church-bells off Lezant Point this morning."

"Well, it might have been fancy," said the officer, putting up his watch, and speaking somewhat impatiently. "I think I have read or heard your story. You have a clergyman, I suppose, if you have no bells, at this goodly village of yours?"

Something sharp in his tone made the hostess think her new customer was displeased, and she remembered what her husband often told her, that it was bad policy to find fault with the locality to which they wished to

attract visitors.   Nevertheless, she was somewhat perplexed what to say in favour of a
minister whom she scarcely knew by sight,
and who did so little for the encouragement
of sociability.

"There is a clergyman, of course, sir; a
resident clergyman," she added, warming a
little as she went on.   "Ours is not like one of
those benighted places across the moors, where,
as I hear travellers say, the minister has put
up blocks of slate and granite to show the
road he has to take over the waste.   North
and east of us there are some horrible places.
Mr. St. Erme is always at home—always to
be found.   His house is away over the headland; not so far if you take the footpath.
Morgan is going to put up a better stile for
ladies.   If we had ladies lodging with us,
they would like to be handy for church.   Mr.
St. Erme has lived a long time at Lezant.   A
very fine dignified gentleman he is, too, in the
pulpit; and Miss St. Erme — not his daughter
— the poor gentleman was never married ; —
she is often in Lezant—not so far as this,
most times; the new building, perhaps, and
the work-people may have scared her; but
she goes about, and is adored among the villagers.   She's almost the only living thing
they do respect and speak about kindly."

The Lieutenant's countenance brightened

up. "There is some grace left among your rude neighbours," he said. "Can you find some one to show me the footpath you mentioned? I should like to see the church nearer."

"Will you go with the gentleman, Owen?" said the pretty young woman, drawing forward the eldest of her shy children. "He knows the way to church as well as any one, and goes to say his catechism and hymns to Miss Mary in the chancel, most Sundays, before service."

The little fellow blushed like a rose, but strode sturdily onward, crossing the street, and taking his way through a narrow alley, behind houses, to a steep flight of steps, which, after a considerable ascent, ended on the top of the cliff. A path across the fields conducted thence to the church, a lonely building, with a stone cross near it. The trees in Mr. St. Erme's grounds, though his house was at some distance, hung over one end of the palings that encircled the graveyard.

While the child, made happy by a small present, retraced his way home, only lingering for a moment or two to gather some flowers, the officer stood still, gazing, with an altered countenance, at the gate leading to the Rectory. Just then, while his head was turned away, a slight form, well known to every inhabitant of Lezant, came towards the spot from the other side of the churchyard. At the sight of a stranger in naval uniform, Mary St. Erme stopped abruptly. The next moment she glided on quickly, passing the little child half-buried among the long grass ; and, when Lieutenant Osborne turned round, the fair apparition — for he had heard no footfall — seemed, to his excited imagination, to have sprung up from the earth.

Though the young girl was very beautiful, there was something inexpressibly mournful in her appearance. It was like the spring landscape, with its leaves and flowers just bursting into bloom, covered with the pitiless snow.

Whether, as he saw that white face rise up before him among the tombs, Osborne really entertained for the moment an idea of supernatural visitation, would be difficult to say ; but his clear, youthful complexion, bronzed by exposure to the weather, paled. As the colour receded there might be traced a marked resemblance in his manly aspect to the shadowy form now clinging wildly to him. As he felt her touch, the warm, living grasp of her slender fingers, the young Lieutenant's cold misgiving passed away ; but still he looked down mournfully and silently on the fair face resting on his bosom.

"I would rather have met you anywhere than here, Mary," he said at last, leading her away from the graves towards the shelter of the trees. "We sailors are always superstitious. I hope it is not an evil omen. How did you know me so quickly?"

Mary St. Erme looked up in his handsome face, to which the colour had returned. "I cannot tell you that, Richard. Something within me and around whispered that you were near me. And then, you are like, very like *him*." Her voice faltered. "Will not every one in this place recognise you?"

"Not easily, with this changed name. I wish it were otherwise, and that they all might know me!" said the young officer, bitterly. "There has been a great mistake made, Mary; and now it is too late to rectify it. I dare say I should find friends, not enemies, here, if I were known. As it is, I live in dread of a discovery which would ruin me in my profession — all I have to live for. If you knew me so quickly, others may, others will detect me; but how could I reject the offer of employment which might bring us together?"

"Do not walk so near the palings!" said Mary, timidly, drawing her companion away from the vicinity of her uncle's garden; "and, oh, Richard, do not speak so loudly! There are such echoes from the hollows in these downs, and at this hour of the afternoon my uncle is generally out of doors. Let us go farther away."

The Lieutenant yielded to her wish, and quitting the churchyard, she led him down by a sequestered path to a combe among the hills, filled with trees, and sloping towards the sea. As he followed her silently, the light form hurrying between the stems of the sighing birches, scarcely rustling the withered leaves by her tread, seemed once more to glide before him like a spirit. At any moment he fancied it might vanish.

"Let me hold you nearer to me, Mary! I scarcely believe that you are real," he said, stopping her when the path widened, and drawing her arm through his own. "Now that I can feel as well as see you, I begin to think myself not quite alone in this cold English world of yours. Tell me, is there any chance of my being acknowledged, if I present myself at the Parsonage? Am I always to be an alien?"

Mary became, if possible, paler than before.

"You must not think of it at present," she answered. "He is changed lately, and for the worse. I never knew him so cold and ungenial. Ever since that most unhappy day when he went to Mr. Helier's, — when the sight of the old house at Woods revived the memory of the past — he has been unlike himself. Till now, though not affectionate, he has always been kind to me."

The tears ran down her cheeks, but the young officer, deeply moved by a name which she had uttered, scarcely heard the last words of her agitated speech.

"Helier!" he said, while a bright, youthful blush sprang to his cheek. "Why do you couple that name with one so hateful to us? What has it to do with Woods?"

"Mr. Helier is the occupant of the Manor Farm now," said Mary, mournfully. "That is the name of Mrs. Fleming's second husband. I have never heard it unconnected with Lord Boscawen's property."

The young man walked along silently, with his eyes cast down, and his thoughts evidently far away. At length, recalling them with an effort, and anxious to hear more, he said,—

"But, Mary, you have not answered my question: What took him there?—to Woods? — Does he often go?—Is he acquainted with Mr. Helier?"

"He knows about as little and as much of him as he does of most of his parishioners," said Mary, sadly. "He leads such a wretched life! — shut up from week to week; — some-

times, from Sunday to Sunday scarcely speaking.   When I hear his voice in church, each
time it sounds to me feebler.   I hardly like to
tell you what took him to Woods.   He did
not mention it to me; but as I went about
the village, among the poor old sick people, I
heard his sad errand.   That place which you
do not like me to name — where the Heliers
live — is accursed.   I need not repeat the
cruel story; but they say that, night after
night, the family are disturbed.   Strange
sights, horrible noises, scare sleep from their
pillows.   For myself, I fear the dead less than
I do the living.   There are strange phantoms
walking the earth — spirits of evil, if you like
to call them so; but they are bad passions
possessing men's hearts; the love of mischief,
— of wickedness, — dark dreams brought on
by remorse for past crimes.   These are the
things that stand by the bedsides, rack the
consciences and awaken the fears of guilty
men; — not disembodied spirits!"

"You speak like one yourself," said the
young man, looking into the pale blue dreamy
eyes of the girl beside him.   "For Heaven's
sake, enlighten me more perfectly.   What
are these ghosts or evil spirits at Woods?   I
would rather hear of them at any other place;
— and what had Mr. St. Erme to do with
them?"

" He thought himself called upon to do
battle against this evil thing," said Mary,
sadly, " and he went manfully to the conflict;
but, oh, Richard, he came back so shaken, so
altered! Except in the church, I have hardly
heard his voice since. He does not sleep or
eat, my poor uncle! He is so terribly changed
that I dare not go near him. This is not the
time to expose him to what, I fear, would be
a severe trial."

" So be it, then!" answered the young
man, sternly, while a dark shade passed over
his usually frank, hopeful face. " I have lived
alone so long, Mary, that family love cannot
be an essential point. Henceforth, as it has
been with me hitherto, I must exist without
it. I cannot expose you to gossip by inter-
views with a stranger. This must be our last,
as it is almost our first meeting.

The girl clung to him fondly. As he felt
the pressure of her small hands, his unwonted
sternness relaxed. He looked down upon her
tenderly, and bent his tall form, as if about to
impress a kiss upon her forehead. Mary St.
Erme did not shrink from him, but a slight
noise among the bushes in the hollow startled
the young man, and made him relinquish his
intention.

" Some one is watching us," he said.
" Wait for me, Mary." Then, plunging into

the brushwood, he came suddenly across an ill-favoured man, halting in his gait, who had the air of a disbanded soldier.

Richard Osborne's haughty looks, as he demanded what he was lurking there for, seemed considerably to alarm him. He looked at the young officer's heated countenance with earnest curiosity, and stumped away, saying that he had lost himself in the thicket, and was trying to find the way back to Lezant.

The Lieutenant did not assist him; but, after watching him out of sight, returned to Miss St. Erme.

"This is a hint for us to be cautious," he said. "That meddling fool will say in the village that he saw us together. Tell me one thing before we part,—In which direction lie Lord Boscawen's woods?"

"Do not go there, Richard!" said Mary, trembling. "It is an evil place for us. The people who dwell there are wild and ill-conducted. Let us avoid them."

The young man did not, for a moment, reply.

"I am not going there," he said; "not, at least, if I can help it. Should duty oblige, I must be like the old man, your uncle — I do not choose to call him mine, since he seems inclined to disown the tie — and not falter. Now, I am going back to the cutter.

But, first tell me, where am I to look to-night for the household lights at Woods? I shall not go the house, but I wish to see them burning."

Mary St. Erme pointed with her finger along the coast, as they stood on the high ground near the church.

" It is further off than you can see from here; and it is a dark, unwholesome place, choked up with trees. I doubt whether, from any distant spot on land or sea, a light at Woods can be discerned. A wild, black creek runs up from the shore, and joins the inland valley, formed by the course of a stream which flows from the moor. This is all I can tell you, for I never walk in that direction; but the seamen at the port will show you where the woods come down to the beach."

Richard Osborne thanked her, gravely, and walked away, not venturing upon a more tender leave-taking than a firm, warm pressure of her trembling hand. He did not immediately return to the harbour, but walked along the cliff, for a considerable distance, to the top of one of its most commanding headlands; then, throwing himself down upon the turf, he took in, with a quick glance, every creek and indentation of the shore.

Only a line darker than the rest marked the situation of the farm at Woods. He saw

where the brook came down from the moor,
and entered a deep combe, within which it
was entirely lost to sight. He could not see
into the recesses of the valley; nevertheless,
he looked for a long time towards the spot,
as if anxious to stamp its memory upon his
heart. Then he rose, and taking the short
cut by which the child had guided him, he
returned to the inn, and to his long-neglected
repast. An hour·afterwards he was on board
his cutter, watching the stars come out in the
clear sky, mirrored in the deep waters of the
narrow creek.

CHAPTER V.

THE Curlew, closely watched by jealous eyes, remained for several days at her moorings in the port of Lezant; while her crew, with such assistance as they could obtain on shore, were busy rectifying some slight damage she was said to have sustained in passing down the Bristol Channel. The trade in slate, which was very brisk, especially in the winter season, when the prevailing winds came off the land and did not ruffle the waves of the estuary, often brought vessels to fetch their cargoes from the small harbour. Near the water's edge, as might be expected, craftsmen were to be found capable of executing the repairs needed for the rigging of the Revenue cutter. The people of Lezant, however, more particularly those belonging to the old village, who did not profit by the custom thus brought to the place, regarded the proceedings of the strangers with distrust; declaring, as they drank their measures of liquor at the Three Crowns, the ordinary gathering-place of the discontented, that the smart new vessel — if, indeed, she wanted overhauling — would have been better refitted at any other port than the one wherein her commander had thought fit to anchor.

Lieutenant Osborne did not appear to trouble himself respecting any remarks that might be made upon the subject. He passed his time pleasantly enough, as it would seem, superintending very diligently the little more than nominal repairs which yet sufficed to give employment to his men; and then spending the remainder of the lengthening spring afternoons and evenings on shore. He patronised the Boscawen Arms liberally, and won golden opinions from the young couple, who had previously begun to despond as to the success of their speculation. Undoubtedly, it was a fair wind for the new inn which had carried the cutter into the harbour.

The young officer's chief amusement consisted in long excursions, which he made on foot and in plain clothes, to every point of interest in the neighbourhood. He was quite mistaken if he thought that these rambles did not attract attention, or that his handsome person was unrecognised. Morgan Price, the landlord of the Boscawen Arms, and his pretty, good-natured wife, often remonstrated with him, telling him that it was foolhardy to go alone, and stay out till dark night on the cliffs and in the deep valleys, with which the moor was indented. He was sure to be an object of suspicion, perhaps of dislike, to the bad people who got their livelihood by smuggling; and stories were told of evil deeds perpetrated by them, when disturbed in their illegal practices; but the Lieutenant did not discontinue his solitary walks, and his frank cheerfulness was not diminished by any apparent consciousness of danger.

One of the places he was most inclined to frequent, and against which his friends at the inn took the greatest pains to warn him, was the course of the stream above the deep-wooded hollow near Lord Boscawen's old Manor-house. In whichever direction Richard Osborne set forth, some secret instinct, either in going or returning, was sure to lead him past the gates of Woods. Nor did he exercise as much discretion on this subject as on some others; for, while he never mentioned the name of St. Erme, or alluded to his interview with Mary, that of Helier was frequently on his lips; and he strove in every way, by direct and indirect interrogatories, to obtain the information he desired.

" The old inn is the place to hear about

Mr. Helier's family:—the Brocks have their custom," said Morgan Price, in answer to one of his guest's numerous questions. " Mr. Helier of Woods never puts up here. I beg your pardon, Captain, but, if I might venture to advise, you wouldn't go near that place. It was past ten o'clock when you came back last night, and my dame was looking out up street half a dozen times. It is not right to be so venturesome."

The officer laughed, but his merriment met with no response.

" They are a desperate gang, those Lezant hill-folk, 'as we call them," continued the young publican; " and their dealings with foreign vessels don't tend to make them better. The less you go nigh them, the safer for you. Keep down here by your vessel, where you 're master; on the quay, or at the Boscawen Arms; even on the open cliffs and downs, where a man can see all round him, and you 'll do well enough: but it 's not only woman's nonsense when my wife says, that among those combes and valleys up country she would not answer for your life."

" You think that the people at Woods Farm have dealings with foreign vessels?" said the Lieutenant, without noticing the caution Price's words conveyed. " Do such craft often put into your harbour? Have

there been any here lately? The Custom-
house authorities had warning, before I left
Bristol, of a suspicious-looking schooner lurking in the Channel."

"Yes, yes! sure enough, you're on the
right tack, sir," said the landlord, significantly.
" La Belle Marie was off Lezant Point five
days ago, and she has not landed her cargo
yet. Perhaps, the Curlew was too near for
her to venture in, and it blew half a gale of
wind from the west. Only a boat pulled in
with a young girl, looking like a foreigner;
at least, my Missus said the cut of her boots
and cloak was French; and she, and two of
the sailors who came with her and left her,
passed our door. The men went off to their
vessel with Lance Fleming the same night."

The Lieutenant listened attentively, and
his fair complexion flushed. "Lance Fleming! that is the son of the last occupant of
Lord Boscawen's farm!" he said, quickly.
" Does he live at Woods? What became of
the foreign-looking young lady who landed
from the schooner?"

Price answered the last question first.
" One of the farm-carts was in the town, and
took her up at the old inn. If she was anything of a lady — and my wife did say she
looked like one — she must have found herself
in strange company at Mother Brock's.

However, she did not stop there more than an hour or so. She's kin to Mr. Helier, who calls himself a Jersey man, but is more French than English; and she comes — so I hear — to teach his daughters manners. They're a queer rough lot to get among."

The young man walked up and down the small parlour uneasily, but he did not speak.

"As for young Fleming, about whom you asked me a question, no one knows much of him. He's not a great deal at Woods, I fancy. John Helier and he don't get on well together. If there's mischief astir, by land or sea, he makes one in it. A wild chap, and a daring one, too. But he's out and out better than his stepfather. People do say Mr. Helier has tried to corrupt him and lead him into bad company, and would be glad to be rid of him on any terms. His mother is a poor weak woman, and would make over everything she has in the world to her husband, though he uses her shamefully, if Lance's rights did not stand in the way. She was scared by her first husband's shocking death, and has been hardly right in her mind since; and the two Helier girls are half-witted. I don't envy the person who has to teach them."

Richard Osborne, who had taken up his cap, as if disinclined to listen to the story to which the landlord alluded, stopped at the last words.

"What will become of her amongst such people? Poor Reine!" he said, unconscious that he was speaking aloud. "I mean," he added, confusedly, aware of his mistake when he saw Price look at him quickly, — "the schooner, La Belle Marie. You think her Captain, the cunning Dutchman, has dealings with Mr. Helier? It looks like it, since he brought his kinswoman from Dinan."

"They won't catch you napping," said Price, approvingly. "So she came from Dinan! — the French schooner, I mean. I thought you knew something more than the rest of us about her. She's often over here, and my belief is, the people at the old inn get all their goods, spirits, and tobacco, that way; yes, and silks and gloves, and many fine things which ladies should be ashamed to wear, without paying the Crown dues, but which they do get duty-free up the country. That raffish soldier with the wooden leg travels about, when custom's slack at the house, selling them to whoever will buy. There must be capital hiding-places at Woods — thickets that a dog could scarce creep through, and slabs of slate and marble that look as if nature had set them up on purpose to cover secrets. Why, where the trade is con-

cerned, the very graves are not held sacred.
There was a time when a great run had been
made. The Custom-house people got scent
of it, and were close upon the men, but
could find nothing; and no wonder. They
couldn't disturb poor people burying their
dead in the churchyard up among the hills —
St. John's in the Wilderness, they call it.
There were the mourners, quite a train of
them, and the coffin; but if they had looked
inside, or under some of the tombstones
which seemed as if they had not been displaced for years and years, what would they
have found there but choice Havannah cigars,
and kegs of rum and brandy above proof!

" One of the gaugers went prying about,
for he smelt a rat; and what became of him
was never known. There was a story got
up that he had crossed the moors, and fallen
into Dozmare Pond. I 'd as soon believe he
was carried away by Tregeagle, the Cornish
giant! Any way there 's a rent in the ground
much nearer the old church, that has gone by
the name of the Gauger's Hole to this day;
and I 've but little doubt, when they found
the poor fellow was likely to be troublesome,
they clapped him into it, and stopped the
pit with just such a slab of slate as lies here,
there, and everywhere about the moor. Half
these idle stories, which fly about the country

like wildfire, are hatched by the smugglers to
further their own aims and ends. I don't
believe the ghosts at Woods are anything but
strapping big fellows, each with a bale of silks
or a cask of spirits under his arm. They
don't want people to be free of the place. It
is Mr. Helier's interest to keep off intruders;
and he wouldn't mind telling a lie or two,
I'll be bound, and has done it a score of
times, to frighten folks off his premises."

"I am inclined to think you are right,"
said Osborne. "Last night, just as it was
getting dusk, it so chanced that I was passing
the gate of the broad avenue leading to the
old Manor-house. The place was dark and
still : such I imagine to be its character. As
I turned to go away, something that I saw
brought involuntarily to my mind the idle
stories you mention, and to which I had been
listening very recently. A tall dark thing—
I could scarcely for some time tell whether it
bore a human form—was rushing about
restlessly to and fro, between the tree stems.
I saw it several times before I felt certain that
it was a man, uttering strange moans, as if in
bodily pain. The noise in that wild place,
after all I had heard, sounded, I must confess,
unreal, unearthly. As quietly as I could, I
unfastened a small gate by the side of the
large one, and entered the avenue. The trees

were set so close together, that it was only in one place that any light penetrated, and the ghost-like creature I was watching turned and saw me, just as I came opposite the opening. He had the advantage over me, for the spot where he stood was in shadow. All I could observe was a tall, dark, shrouded form; and it did not stop to question, but fled or vanished so quickly, that I could almost have believed it sank into the earth, after uttering a wild cry of alarm. I have thought since that these spectral sounds, and the whole theatrical effect, might have been got up to terrify me, as it certainly would have done any timid person."

"You should not go there, Mr. Osborne!" said Price. "Harm will come of it, I lay my life, if you do. Why, scarce a man in this town would do what you did; and I'll be bound most of them would say you had seen the ghost. I'm not superstitious myself, but still I think it would be tempting Providence. There's something in these stories, take my word for it; and if it is not what they would have us believe, it may be worse."

The landlord of the Boscawen Arms would have been grievously disappointed if he had known that the immediate result of his well-meant expostulation was to take Lieutenant Osborne more directly in the path of danger than ever. That very afternoon, the inmates of the taproom of the Three Crowns, and of the tottering houses on the naps, watched the fair, handsome youth take his fearless way past their doors, and up among the wild hills that shut in the upper village. As he strolled along, glancing quickly from right to left, and now and then whistling or humming the gay tune of a French barcarolle, the men eyed him stealthily, cursing his boldness, and wondering what brought him and his swift-sailing vessel into their waters. Above the town Osborne turned off by short cuts, which were now familiar to him, and crossed the down till he struck into a path which brought him to the gates of Woods. He did not go in, but after lingering for a brief space gazing down the sombre avenue, with here and there a narrow streak of sunlight stealing across it, and the old house at the farther end in deep shadow — waiting long enough, in short, to observe that no person was about—the young officer ascended towards the source of the stream which came dashing down from the moor.

There was less animation in his gait, now, and he did not sing or whistle. Something of disappointment rested on his features, yet still he walked on, keeping near the water, until he came to the spot where the spring gushed out of the side of the hill, nearly a

couple of miles above the house he had passed.
A few bushes and tufts of gorse fringed the
pool formed by the first outbreak of the
water ; then its course narrowed, and became
defined by sharp ledges of slate .and steep
blocks of granite, over which clung brambles
and blackberry briers. He could trace the
brook all the way down till it plunged into
the dark chasm filled by Lord Boscawen's
woods.

On the open moor, just above the spring,
surrounded by crumbling walls and a few old
headstones, on which the inscriptions were
mostly effaced, stood a very ancient church,
built of granite, and roofed with pale bluish-
coloured slate. The services had long been
discontinued, but the sacred edifice was kept
standing, and some few families still buried
their dead in the small graveyard. Lance
Fleming's father—the man said to have been
murdered near Woods—lay under the green
turf freshened by the stream which passed
close under the angle of the wall nearest to
the chancel. On this tomb the inscription
was not obliterated, but it set forth only the
name and age of the deceased, and the date
of the year in which he perished. His widow
had not, like most other mourners, resorted to
Holy Writ for expressions commemorative of
her grief, of pious hope, or of the merits of the

departed. Neither was there any account given
of the manner in which his life ended. In the
corner near his grave, some scathed-looking
willow and alder - bushes made a perpetual
sighing, as the wind, always strong upon the
moor, whistled among their branches, and the
tall flags through which the brook gushed
along, shivered in the blast.

The young man's countenance, grave previously, became sad as he looked at the tomb
and read the brief record engraven upon it.
He did not stop long, but with a sort of
shudder — for he was not as free from super-
stition as the landlord of the Boscawen Arms
— he came quickly out through the little gate
by which he had entered a few moments before, and stood with his usual earnest gaze
marking the flow of the stream downward, as
far as it continued within view, and the general aspect of the wild hills spreading out on
every side. After his survey was over, he
walked on thoughtfully, alongside of a watercourse into which a portion of the brook was
artificially conducted, probably for the purpose of supplying some of the works which in
this county, rich in mineral wealth, were sure
to be found at no remote distance.

Osborne had not gone far before he perceived that his proceedings were closely
watched by a very old man riding a

donkey, who had come down the opposite
side of the watercourse, apparently to meet
him. The young sailor was too true and
kind-hearted not to feel respect for age, and
he touched his cap, and bade the old fellow
good-day cordially, but without stopping.
After a little while, seeing that the runlet was
conducting him into a still more barren and
less interesting country, Osborne retraced his
steps. The man on the donkey turned about
also, following close, and keeping a sharp
look-out upon him.

The Lieutenant's curiosity was awakened,
and dismissing the sombre thoughts with
which, since leaving the churchyard, his mind
had been occupied, he slackened his pace, and
allowed the old man to overtake him. The
donkey trotted up briskly, incited by sound
kicks from its rider's heels, as well as by the
prospect of company, which is always agreeable to dumb animals. At first, the old man's
dialect was so peculiar that Osborne hardly
understood his Cornish idiom; but, as they
went on together, the difficulty lessened.

He was set, Osborne gathered from his
discourse, to mind the water, for which he
received a small salary from Lord Boscawen,
paid half-yearly by his steward. Not the
waste water, he said, contemptuously, as the
young sailor's eye followed the glad, free

current dashing along in its own wild way, and flinging showers of foam on the daisies and grass; but that which was penned up between sharp-pointed stones, and led down by a sort of miniature canal to the neighbouring works. That was worth looking after! and sometimes the shepherd lads used to play tricks with it and stop it, till he was set on to keep the channel clear of obstruction.

The place was so wild and lonely, with no trace of man's toil or presence, save the little church falling into ruin, the mouldering gravestones and the narrow watercourse, that the precautions thought necessary by the old man appeared almost ludicrous. Osborne fancied he must have misunderstood his account of the nature of his employment, and questioned him farther, remarking at the same time that a long residence in a foreign country, where he had received nearly the whole of his education, made it difficult for him occasionally to comprehend the dialects spoken in various parts of England.

"I can make out what ye say tu I well enoo'," said the old man, wonderingly. "What hinders ye to follow I?—It's good Saxon-English ye speak—not the language of the king that had a castle once on our carns, and died by the Crooked River—down to Sloven Bridge yonder. Ye be terrible plain-spoken—not like the foreigners tu 'Oods. I can't tell what they say—feckless girls!—not if they screech tu I; but his lordship, I minded what he told I, when he fished the brook, and you're just like he—just such another. Were you reared in France, did ye say, like the folks tu Helier's?"

The old man put his hand behind his ear, as if he were troubled with deafness, but his sharp looks did not seem to belong to one so afflicted. Osborne answered with seeming carelessness, which also was affected,—

"Are there any French people living at Woods? I dare say they would like to see a person from their own country. A month ago I was in Brittany."

"French people? Aye, aye, if ye like them! French enough, are they—tu 'Oods! They eat snails, and frogs, and lizards out of the green nooks in the walls; ivats, we call 'em. There's the Master, he's too French for I!—and the Missus—no one knows what she is: then the ramshackle girls, they've French names and French manners. They're the scampishest creatures I ever see'd; my donkey knows better. They were up at the water-course only yesterday—bless 'em, pretty dears! and nothing would serve but they'd make dirt puddings and choke up the channel. Such a mess as they made of it; and throwing pebbles and stones, and screeching with laughter when I rode down upon them! The young lady that was with 'em was more civil; but we'd a hantle of trouble. She sat over by the thorn-bush yonder," the old man went on, his grey eyes twinkling as he perceived how attentively Osborne was listening. "She didn't speak French tu I, though, but English, mighty pretty; as well as I do, or you, for that matter: but she said she'd come from foreign parts lately; and more unlikely things have happened than her liking to hear something about them."

"Shall you see these ladies again?" said Osborne, as he bestowed a handsome gratuity, equal to a quarter of his lordship's salary, upon the crafty old man, who eyed him and the coin alternately with intense interest.

"Well, I might and I mightn't! I think I'm like enough tu;" said he of the donkey, when he saw the amount of the present. "Which inn does your honour put up at? I'm thinking it will be the Boscawen, if you're stopping in the place."

Osborne hastily twisted off a leaf from his pocket-book, and wrote a few words hurriedly in pencil upon it.

"Can I trust you, my old friend, to give this to the young lady you saw yesterday with

Mr. Helier's daughters?" he said, colouring.
" I do not wish to go to Woods at present,
and I may not be so fortunate as to meet her.
My commission will not interfere with your
charge of the water?"

" No, no! the water wastes off down to
'Oods; and though I don't make a point of
following it, I might ride after it now and
then. The ass will carry me, never fear, sir!
The young lady shall have the note, if you
give it tu I. It's useless folding it. How
would a poor fellow that can't read his book,
nor sign his name, make out the writing?"

The chance seemed too favourable to be
let slip by the young lover. Nevertheless, it
was not without some misgiving that Richard
Osborne watched the roguish leer in the old
man's eye, as he edged his donkey near
enough to receive the missive. Not feeling
inclined for further parley, he bade him good-
bye civilly; and this time, satisfied with his
day's work, his new friend did not try to
accompany him longer.

Osborne walked on quickly, somewhat
dissatisfied with himself for the step he had
taken; and fearing lest he should have exposed Reine to misconstruction in her new
home. If, however, he might judge by his
faithfulness to Lord Boscawen, the strange

old fellow deserved to be trusted; for the Lieutenant, whenever he looked back from his path by the side of the water, could perceive that its trusty guardian had moved on far enough to keep him in sight; and the man was sitting upon his donkey, relieved against the sunset sky, when Osborne turned his head for the last time before he desisted from following the stream at the gates of Woods.

CHAPTER VI.

On the ascending slope at the back of the
Manor-house, partly sunny, partly shaded,
and surrounded by high old crumbling walls,
rent and riven, and then again knit together
by the growth of ivy, with which the lapse of
years had covered them, was what might once
have been a productive orchard; but the trees
now bore no other crop than long wreaths of
pendent moss. Here and there a bunch of
pink-and-white blossoms peeped through the
silvery beards of the ancient trees; but the
fruit never ripened; and when the wind rose
it played with the long grey fringes, and
whistled through the otherwise naked boughs,
with an eerie sound.

When the sun shone bright, and the grass
beneath was soft and green, as now, after the
winter rains, starred with daisies, and, at the
roots of the old grey trunks, with primroses
and violets, the place was warm and sheltered.
In the corner under the wall stood Leah
Scriven, the housekeeper's beehives; and the

air was full of the sound of the busy insects'
humming. Showers of white blossoms, frail
as snow-flakes, hung lightly on the dark spikes
of some old blackthorn-bushes, which had
grown into straggling trees, shooting out their
branches wildly, and often pushing a way for
themselves through the wall; and springing
up in the niches of the stone-work, in the
corner where the hives were placed, grew
dark, rich-scented gillyflowers, round which
the bees were circling gladly.

Across the orchard, reaching from trunk
to trunk of the moss-grown apple-trees, were
rope lines, on which Reine was busily hanging out her French caps, with their long lappets edged with narrow lace, and her fine
muslin cuffs and collars. No wonder that, as
she placed them in the sunshine, the girl was
singing; or that the words which came to her
lips belonged, not to her present life, but to
the sunnier land she had quitted. Homely
as her occupation might appear, there was in
Reine's air and manner something that im-
parted to it a sentiment. Her quick movements were all graceful, whether bending to
gather a flower, or stepping on a fallen stone
to reach the line. The lively, easily-roused
sensibilities of her nature, were called into
play by the warm sunshine, the incense-
bearing morning atmosphere, even by the

touch of the delicate embroidery wrought by
the fingers of merry girls, like herself, in
Breton farms and cottages.

In her song, too, though it was a mirthful
one, there breathed at intervals a deeper tone;
her eyes, as they wandered over the nearer
view, seemed to grow darker, and then suddenly to dilate, as she fixed them on some
spot in the distance. It might be a birch-
stem standing out beyond its companions in
the thicket, a slab of slate or granite boulder,
such as frequently broke the long line of
woodland. Be the object what it might on
which her eye momentarily rested, Reine's
cheek would flush, her breath fail her; the
song stopped; and then, over the blushing
face and sparkling glance would come a
shadow, in the glad free tones a check, a
mournful fall, which told that the impatient
spirit was chafing over the disappointment
of some cherished expectation; one of those
many bright hopes of youth which the breath
of flowers and the warm gush of sunshine gift
with richer life, but which, in their over-
throw, make the bright things blooming
around the dreamer seem to perish with
them.

Unobservant as he was, on most occasions,
of the young guest at Woods, Lance Fleming
stopped to look at her, as Reine stood for a

moment with her hand over her eyes, gazing wistfully out, as she had done twenty times before, that morning, into the dusky wood-land. Nothing was to be seen but the dark boughs and trunks of the trees, closing in thicker and thicker as the ground fell towards the ravine. Lance had his hands full of busi-ness — real, practical, unmistakeable, earnest business, which could not well brook delay; nevertheless, he did not pass the little gate leading into the orchard, but stood hesitating, looking at Reine as if more than half inclined to speak to her.

"Eh bien?" said the girl, laughing, as she broke off her song. "I beg your pardon; I forgot you do not understand me: but everything comes to me in French this morn-ing. This warm air is like Brittany. Will you not find that great rough jacket too sultry?"

The girl looked earnestly as she spoke at Lance's seamanlike garb, and her eyes again grew dark and thoughtful.

"Out to sea there is a roughish wind blowing now," said Lance. "I dare say it blew through and through your thin clothes when you came in the schooner. What sort of passage had you? I suppose Jacob Mohr speaks French as well as that German gib-berish. Had you any talk together?"

" Mynheer speaks our beautiful language like a native," said Reine, her cheeks glowing with animation at the mention of her absent friend. " His vessel, of which he is so proud —La Belle Marie—ah! she skims the seas like a bird! Well! he built her on our sandy dunes: the timbers of her keel were laid in my father's yard. The pretty name she bears he told me to give it to her, when she was launched. Many times I have listened to tales he told me about this coast; which, he said, was like our own Armorique —once, perhaps, they were united. Now, the great sea flows between; but there are curious churches buried deep in shifting sands, and forests submerged below high-water mark; beaches raised by the action of the sea, and left forty or fifty feet above its present level. He has visited all countries, and can relate wonders of what he has seen under the tropics, and in those icy, northern regions, where daylight lasts through what are the darkest hours with us. Ah, he is a great traveller, le Capitaine Mohr! and he carries the same kind heart with him everywhere."

Lance listened attentively.

" I never heard so much about Jacob Mohr before," he answered; " but I know that he is a good fellow, though, generally, he does not say a great deal. He brought the dog for me at some trouble to himself, when I wanted to have one of the breed. What took him first to Brittany?"

"Ah! that is a long while ago. I do not think that I can tell you. Mynheer does not like his affairs to be spoken about," said the French girl, hesitating. "He was acquainted with some of our people, and they trusted him entirely. I believe he brought a cargo of rich merchandise, which was consigned to my father. C'est assez! I do not comprehend these matters. Mynheer will tell you himself what he thinks it proper you should know."

"Good day, then!" said Lance, as he turned to go. Some indefinable suspicion made Reine draw nearer to him; when she noticed, for the first time, a paper, which he was twisting impatiently in his fingers.

"Qu'est-ce que c'est?" she said. "Let me see that writing! Is it French? Ah! it is not worth while to take that to Captain Mohr. I will tell you the meaning directly."

She put her hand over the gate, but Lance held back.

"No, no!" he answered, "Mademoiselle, no need to trouble you. This is one of our smuggling secrets. Jacob Mohr must have picked up French enough to read it. For

my part, I wish there was no language spoken
or written but English."

He went off abruptly, forgetting to call
his dog, which was crouching at Reine's feet,
half hidden by her dress; for Bouffe had not
yet become attached to his new master, and
preferred her company. Lance was hardly
ever at home, and Reine was sorry she had
not asked him for news of the cutter lying,
she had heard, in the port of Lezant. The
women of the family cared nothing about
such matters, and she felt afraid to question
her dark-browed, silent kinsman.

Mr. Helier, she knew, must have seen the
vessel, for he had attended market, and the
few persons who came on business to the
farm said that the village was full of talk
about the sailors; but the master of the house
drew in his chair to the table as silently as
usual when he came home, and Reine, with
her heart beating and her colour rising and
going each moment, with the thoughts that
tried to frame themselves into speech, and
died away unuttered, wanted courage to put
any inquiry to him.

He went out again directly after the repast was finished; and when she passed him
in the passage, on her way to her own room,
he looked strangely pale and haggard. The
old, faded, washed-out pictures of the Bos-

cawens, staring down from the walls, were
not more ghastly. Nevertheless, could the
girl have guessed what the form was like
which, an hour before, had crossed his path
in the moonlit avenue, she would have faced
it fearlessly !

If the young foreigner could not flatter
herself that she had made any impression
upon Lance Fleming, his dog was much more
open to the spell of her beauty and winning
ways. One secret of her influence was, that
Reine always addressed him in French ; and
Bouffe would prick up his ears, and shake the
crisp curls of his coat, when he heard the
sound of her voice. She followed him now
by the side of the stream ; stopping sometimes,
and throwing in bits of stick and pebbles,
which the water-spaniel plunged after immediately, and brought to her feet.

Though the dog would use all sorts of
mute intreaties to make her throw twigs and
branches into the running water, Bouffe never
enforced the argument by barking. He was
as silent as Mr. and Mrs. Helier ; and considering the want of animation in the rest of
her companions, Reine often wished that the
dog would be more loquacious. Those lonely
woods, where her own footstep, rustling
among the leaves, was almost the only sound
heard, would have been enlivened by the

short sharp yelp with which a spaniel chases a rabbit; but the stream, rippling along its pebbly bed, was more noisy than the smuggling Captain, Jacob Mohr's favourite.

In those dark depths of foliage Reine Helier would wander for hours, feeling less alone than in her kinsman's gloomy house. There was one spot where an immense mass of slate seemed to stop the water; but the stream had worn for itself a path under the stone, and fell, with one bold leap, into a wilderness of brambles. The girl did not know that in this wild place, years afterwards, women would build for themselves, like the wild birds, a nest of boughs, and leaves, and sods; and, having entered in, for whatever strange grief or cruelty that might have disturbed their reason, abide there till both perished. There was no such tradition, then, among the many strange tales told by the peasantry about Boscawen's Grange; but when she had got thus far, Reine stopped and shuddered. The dampness of the atmosphere, full of the spray from the cascade which hung on every leaf, chilled her.

She would not have ventured farther, if Bouffe had not sprung down a rocky step or two in the bank, and looked back, as if asking her to come with him; but she soon half repented of her acquiescence. The brawl of the stream, hidden from her by the boughs, confused her, and she feared to miss her footing on the rock, which was slippery from the wet green moss covering its surface.

Aslant across the edge of the Keeve, or bason of granite which received the principal fall of the water, another slab had lodged, which broke the line of the cascade, but the stream found its way through a cleft in the rocks, throwing sparkles and showers of foam around. Reine, as she stood in the cool shadow of the dell beneath, could not help watching the dog scrambling along the ridges of the bank, snuffing and scratching the soil, and thrusting his nose into every interstice of the rock, as if he were tracking some animal of which he was in pursuit. Not the smallest live creature, however, was visible. The cascade, seen through the natural arch of rock, as it fell into the Keeve, and then, like a thin vapoury curtain, into the pool below, the waving of the branches overhead in the tangled ravine, were the only moving objects within view.

Reine had to call the dog several times before he would give up his vain search. At last, tired of the solitary aspect of the place, almost frightened, she turned to retrace her steps, when, as she mounted the steep ascent among the bushes, she was startled by a cry of pain or terror, and then, mingling with the rustling of the leaves and the sigh of the wind, affrighted weeping. The dog had run quickly on before her, and when she reached the top-most step she saw that Bouffe had found his master.

Close by the edge of the cascade, with the green shadow of the water and the refracted light sent back by the foliage which inter-cepted the sunbeams, making her pale thin face quite ghastly, was the youngest of Mr. Helier's children, and with her the half-brother, of whom both the girls stood in awe. Lance's arm was passed round the little crea-ture's waist. He was holding her forcibly, and her struggles and entreaties showed that, if he had let her go, she would have been out of sight in an instant.

" Read it, I say, you stupid, foolish little thing ! I don't want to hurt you ; " Lance was saying. " What harm will the green water do you ? you should not have run down here, if you were afraid of it. No, I have not time for another chace. I won't let you stir till you tell me what is written on this paper."

" Oh, I can't, I won't ! Laissez-moi ! " exclaimed the child, trembling with passion or terror. " Are those snakes ?—look how they glide, and twist, and coil ! Oh, they must be

alive! This water is so cold—I wish I had
not come here—that you had not seen me.
Oh, how you hurt me!"

"Listen to me, Victoire," said Lance, se-
riously. "Those are not snakes, but the
green flakes of the water gliding down a deep
dark pit. Must I throw you after them, or
will you translate to me the few French words
on this page? You can do it, I know, if you
like. You and Zélie are chattering French
half the day to each other."

The child threw back her long disordered
hair from her eyes, which were red with crying. She seemed to have made up her mind
to obey her half-brother, and put her hand up
for the paper. As the shining gleam of the
cascade, almost underneath which she was
standing, fell on her wet cheeks, and glittered
in the mischievous beam that shot from under
her dark lashes, Reine saw that she was not
sincere. There was no goodness in that smile;
nevertheless, it deceived the youth, and he let
go the paper.

In an instant, and with a gesture of pas-
sionate malice, the little girl flung it, with all
her might, after crumpling it up into a ball,
into the water.

"There—go!—you will never plague me
more—no one can read the crooked letters—
the wild waters may make play with them.

They are down, down in the deep hole, where it is all darkness!"

Reine's nature was so different from that of the spiteful child, that the expression of annoyance on Lance's face would alone have prompted her to wish that the writing he wanted to decipher should not be destroyed. But as she watched the fluttering scroll, some other feeling, to herself inexplicable, made her long to preserve it. Pointing to the paper, she said to Bouffe the one word which acted like magic when spoken by the Captain of La Belle Marie—" *Cherche!* " and Bouffe, as he would have sprung into the green sea-waves that lashed the side of the schooner, dashed into the watercourse, and arrested the paper, just as it was gliding over the ledge.

Lance turned at the sound, and the moment his hold upon her was relaxed, Victoire, clapping her hands for joy, fled from the spot. Meanwhile, Bouffe, dripping with water, brought his prize to Reine.

The girl's fingers trembled as she unwrapped and smoothed the paper. She held it fast, and her cheek flushed joyfully when she saw that only the outside was wetted.

" It is mine!" she said; " why did I not have it sooner?   Ah, Bouffe! but for you I should not hold it now.   Why did Monsieur Fleming not give me my letter?"

"It is not a letter," said Lance, "only a leaf torn out of a book—not meant for you, nor perhaps for any one, but it is important to us—to Captain Mohr, I mean. Will you tell me, word for word, the meaning of what is written here about the time when the Revenue cutter is to sail out of harbour? The rest is nothing."

Reine's face flushed crimson, and then became deadly pale, as she looked at the paper, and read the few guarded words in which Richard Osborne bade her meet him on the beach, near the ruins of Arthur's Castle, on the evening of the day before the one on which she became aware of the appointment.

"The Curlew — that is the vessel which came into Lezant port last Sunday,—will sail again with the flood-tide — la haute marée,— Saturday — that is to-day, at six o'clock. Why, that is this very afternoon! — It is too late. — Méchant! why did I not get this sooner?"

Lance laughed at her vehemence.

"That is enough for us," he said. "It is sharp practice between Mynheer and the Revenue vessels. Half-an-hour would make all the difference in landing the goods."

He left Reine standing, like the image of despair, by the waterfall, and went quickly

back to the house, and to the portion of it
which had been his ever since his own father's
death or murder.

A broad flight of rough, uneven, wooden
steps led up to his bedroom, which, like the
rest at Woods, was large and comfortless.
Most of the articles it contained bespoke the
hardy, erratic habits of their possessor; others
were entirely unconnected with his pursuits.
Great sacks of corn were piled up on the landing, and in the corner next his door were
heavy cart-whips, and part of the broken tire
of the wheel of a waggon.   Inside Lance's
apartment were miscellaneous stores — garments fitted for all weathers, tarpaulins for
boats, oars, guns, fishing-rods and imple-
ments, with a suspicious-looking keg, flanked
by an enormous jar of bran, out of which,
when he entered, Leah Scriven was filling a
copious measure, as she stood, with her back
to the door, half in and half out of a large
cupboard.

.   Lance took no notice of her, but began
hastily plunging into a hand-valise some articles of clothing which he extracted from a
drawer. The woman, turning round, watched
his every movement.

"Are you going away?" she said, coming
behind him, after a few moments. "Let me

pack for you. What things do you want?
Why, Lance, you are but just come back to
us!"

"I have been here long enough," said
Lance. "Let me do it for myself; no one
else can tell what I want. Bid them saddle
the bay mare, and don't sit up. I shall not
be back to-night."

"Stay at home, my boy!" said Leah,
affectionately. "You do yourself no good by
these wanderings. Where have you been
these last three days?"

"On the sea," said Lance, pulling off his
neck-cloth, and dipping his face into a basin of
cold water. "If it were not for my mother,
I should not come back at all."

"There's some grace in that," said the
woman, regarding him compassionately, while
his handsome face glowed, more from anger
than from the immersion. "Shall I tie you
on a clean neckerchief? There's one I ironed
ready in the box. What are you fumbling
with it for?—pulling it all out of the creases!
Let me fold it."

Leah's countenance changed as, snatching
the neck-tie from him unceremoniously, she
discovered the cause of his incapacity. Lance's
hand was cut and bleeding.

"Mercy on us, Master Lance!" she said,
half crying, "what have you gone and done

to yourself? Why will you, a gentleman born,
choose to consort with your inferiors? Be
sure you'll come to the wall. Look at your
fingers, that were straight and smooth like
his, and now are swelled like the louts in
the farmyard! Have you been fighting with
them?"

"Nonsense!—it is nothing," said Lance,
impatiently. "One of the casks on board the
schooner got loose and bruised me. Now,
listen! One of these nights you may very
likely hear noises. Don't be foolhardy, but
lock the French girl into her room if she
seems troubled with curiosity. No need,
either, to look too sharp after the cellar keys
and the stores in the larder. I may bring
company home with me."

"Aye, aye! like enough;—that was said
like *him!*" the old woman answered mournfully. "Only mind my words, Lance. I
should not care for sitting up; no, nor for
seeing you spend your substance on what the
preacher says isn't bread, if the company you
brought home were gentlefolk. Your father,
in his best days, spent his money like a lord,
and he always had the look of one: so have
you, for that matter, when you don't neglect
yourself. There is not one of his lordship's
family in the gallery — your own blood relations — that mightn't be proud to own you,

if you did not let yourself down to consort
with these smugglers, and the publicans who
deal with them. These Dutch skippers, smelling of Hollands and Nantes! Faugh, I wonder at you! When he was your age, your
father came down here with Lord Boscawen,
who was trying to raise a troop of yeomanry,
and not one of them rode like young Fleming.
He was a finer man than my lord by half!"

"Enough of this, Leah!—Don't speak to
me of my father!" said Lance. "He was a
different man before he died. I hate these
old stories. If it were not for the friends I
have made for myself, I should be a beggar.
Whence comes my independence — wealth
(for I have money) — but from these Dutch
skippers you despise? Mynheer is more of a
gentleman than you think, and who knows
but I may be Lord Boscawen yet!"

He went out laughing, after letting the
woman, who had been his father's servant,
apply to his hand some homely unguent, for
which she again dived deep into the recesses
of the cupboard.

There was no sign of disturbance in
Reine's manner, except that her cheeks glowed,
and her eyes had a bright spark gleaming
under their long lashes, while she sat with
Leah during the afternoon, helping her to
finish her task of needlework. Leah must

have been more or less than woman to be able to resist all the efforts made to please her.

Like most of the rooms on the ground-floor of the old house, that where Reine and the housekeeper were sitting together was much darkened by trees, which, as the sun declined, threw long shadows across the floor. The rooks circled round their nests, cawing noisily as they fed their young broods. The large cuckoo-clock flew open, and the bird came out to tell the hour. Reine looked up when she heard it.

"Come! it will do. We have worked for a long time," she said, crossing the room and leaning over the woman's chair. "Your poor eyes will ache. If there is more to be done, I will sit up to-night and finish it. Let us now take a little walk together. How long is it since you have been at Lezant?"

"Long enough, ma'amselle," said the housekeeper, rubbing her eyes after she had taken off her spectacles. "It must be the glasses that try my sight. I never was much of a walker. Let me see —'tis nigh upon six weeks since I were down to Lezant town. Mrs. Brock owes for the butter;—but 'tis no great matter."

"Would it not be better to settle it? See how prettily the sunshine falls through the trees! On the high ground it is light still when here it is almost night. My eyes pain me, too!" said Reine, passing her white hand over her brow. " Surely it is dark, this evening, sooner than usual."

"No, no; it is just the same," said the woman, who was not ill-natured, looking at her compassionately. " One day is like another here. Well, it must be dull for a young creature like you. I don't think you have been out of these dark woods since you came. It's no wonder if you're tired and want a change; so, for once, I don't mind humouring you."

Reine was soon ready, and had even to wait for her companion while she put on her Sunday gown and shawl, and her black silk bonnet. The young French lady straightened it for her, and pinned her on a fresh collar with her usual nicety, in spite of her own impatience to set out. It was more difficult for her to restrain her anxiety, and keep pace with the elderly woman, who, as she had said, was no great walker, when they got upon the downs, and saw how fast the sun was declining westward. By the time they reached the top of the straggling street, one side' of it was in deep shadow.

The light, which had partially gone off the houses, shone full on the nap opposite the

Three Crowns, where a blooming apple-tree, covered with pink-and-white blossoms, stood in the middle of a plot of garden-ground. It was fit, the housekeeper said, for a crown for a bride.

Mrs. Brock was standing at her door, and curtseyed with much deference to Reine and her companion.

" It's but seldom we see you so far from home, Mrs. Scriven. Surely, you give yourself too little recreation. I hope the walk's not been too much for you. And the young lady—I'm proud to see her. There's our little account to settle for the butter, and the inn is as quiet as your own parlour. I'd be happy to make you some tea, if you'd condescend to taste it."

Mrs. Scriven, though she declined the proffered refreshment, went into the house with the woman, while Reine sat down on a stone seat in the porch.

Near the door a few persons were sitting round a table conversing, but in so low a tone that the girl outside heard nothing of what they said. She was watching the small portion of the harbour visible between the houses, which just opened as if on purpose to afford her a glimpse of the mast of the cutter. The Curlew was not gone from Lezant yet.

Presently, the talk of the men grew louder,

and caught her attention. One of them was saying,—

"So, the cutter is to float out with the tide? She's got every stick about her taut and trim, and is as smart as new paint can make her. They've split the ropes and spliced them, six times over. I'd give a good deal to know what's kept her here so long."

"It's not such snug lying in Lezant port when the wind sets up the creek, and the sea is roaring through the blow-holes," observed another. "Her officer's a stranger, and don't know the coast. I hear the Lieutenant spends half his time on shore."

"He's not much of an officer," said the lame soldier, contemptuously. "Six foot two, without shoes, did ye say, master? No, nor five foot ten, either! Our old Passon, though he stoops, is a head taller. He's nothing to speak of in the way of being a gentleman. Why, if he was the least like it, would he stop down to the Boscawen, hand-and-glove with that collier mate, Morgan Price? 'Taint likely!"

"Is it the schooner he's looking for?" said a man, leaning over the table. "He's a-top of every hill in the country, spying out to sea with his glass, and questions all he comes across. There's not a creek or cranny he hasn't searched while the cutter was laid up. Mynheer will be tired of waiting, and go back to Holland without landing his cargo."

" Never you fear, masters! There's other fish for a fine young captain to fry besides looking after smuggling schooners," the lame man remarked, significantly, as he set down a fresh jug of foaming malt. " Every lad has his lass, and the one he's courting lives like a bird in a nest, t'other side of our old Passon's evergreens. Don't let feyther hear us — he'd say 'twas downright blasphemy; but, as sure as I'm alive, I saw the Lieutenant and Miss St. Erme walking together in the hollow by Combe Pyne, last Sunday. She was crying, too; and I won't swear he didn't kiss her. Any way, he threatened to lay his stick across my back for spying after them."

The old man caught his son's jeering accents, though low. He rose, with the aid of his stick, and came to the opening left by the curtain.

" I won't have such words spoken!" he said. " Here, you, my old dame, and that precious young rascal, Andrew, listen! The angels in heaven are not purer than my dear young lady. If I were in my grave, I'd rise up when I heard her slandered. I'll shut up the public if this kind of talk goes on longer."

" I wish the Lieutenant had cudgelled you,

you graceless young reprobate!" said Dame
Brock, angrily. "Leave off fretting the old
man. What matters it to you or to me what
folks are courting, to make you speak against
the real gentry? Mr. St. Erme's no great
customer, certainly; but he don't go to the
Boscawen for what he wants. Let his
Reverence's family be!"

"I don't care about him," answered the
soldier, vindictively; "but the man that
threatens me is my enemy. I've my reasons
for watching the officer of the cutter; and if I
find him with a lass, be she gentle or simple,
alone in dark woods, and get a stick laid
across my back for presuming to look at them,
I know what to think about it. I'm not the
only person that saw them together. They
were watched in the churchyard, and through
the combe in the hills. Folks say 'twas to see
her he dropped anchor in Lezant harbour, and
that he's mortally afraid of the old Passon,
and daren't show himself at the house. That
doesn't look much like the gentleman! He'll
get nobody but Morgan Price to speak to his
character in these parts."

The housekeeper was now ready, having
settled her business with Mrs. Brock; but
Reine had quite lost the eagerness she had
previously manifested to continue their walk.
She steadily refused to go to the new shop

near the water-side, which was patronised by
the cutter people, and where, she was assured,
she could match her fine sewing-cotton;
saying it was useless to try, and that it
was too late. Just then, there rose slowly
above the low buildings by the quay, seen
through the narrow opening between the
houses, the white sails of the vessel which had
lain for a week in the harbour, and was now
putting out to sea.

"You have no time to lose if you'd like to
see the cutter sail out of the basin," said Dame
Brock, who had come into the porch. "It's
no new sight to me; but strangers think a
good deal of seeing the sailing-craft tack and
shift ballast as they creep out of the port. I
shouldn't wonder if they ran her on the rocks.
She is a Government vessel, and never was in
our waters before."

"Trop tard!" the French girl murmured,
as they left the inn: then, seeing that the gate
of the garden-ground on the nap stood open,
she ran up the slope, past the blooming apple-
tree, to the top of the bank, where a seat was
placed which afforded a view of the harbour.
Leah did not follow her; and Reine stood
alone, watching, in the bitterness of her heart,
the vessel, which she knew to be her lover's,
dexterously threading the narrow strait, under
the gaze of numbers of the townspeople.

Her breath came short when she saw the waves dashing against the great rocks at the mouth of the creek ; but the Curlew passed safely between them ; then, setting all the sail she could carry, with wind and tide in her favour, she scudded rapidly past the bluff headlands towards Bude Haven.

CHAPTER VII.

ON the third evening following the departure
of the Revenue cutter the village of Lezant
woke up from its torpitude. Instead of idly
lounging on the naps, pipe in hand, or
skulking behind house-doors and window-
blinds, watching the Lieutenant as he passed,
with a quick, firm step, through their street,
the denizens of the place were all on the alert.
Boats were putting off and coming in with
no attempt at concealment; and men with
passions all on flame, ready to strike down any
opposer of their lawless traffic, were helping
to unlade the goods, and passing them from
hand to hand.

These receivers of contraband articles—
for not one of the bales and casks had paid
duty to the Crown—were all from the upper
inland village, or from places far away among
the green hills; stern, hardy peasantry from
scattered hamlets, or the more depraved inhabitants of the crumbling dwellings perched
on the rocky terraces, and alongside of the

rugged causeway which passed the door of the Three Crowns.

The old hostelry had all the custom this evening, and the new inn, recently so thronged, was now dark and silent. Not a soul was to be seen about the Boscawen Arms, and at an early hour the shutters of the lower rooms were put up, and the front door made fast. Of all the riotous crowd on sea and land, there was not likely to be one who would cross the threshold which had been so popular with the crew of the cutter.

It was better not to show themselves, the young publican said to his trembling wife, as she sat listening, with her baby in her arms, to the wild uproar on the quay; much the best not to see what was going forward. If they could not prevent it, they would at all events keep a clear conscience, so as to be able to show their faces honestly, and say they had no share in that night's work, if the Lieutenant questioned them about it.

Deeply shadowed by the black masses of the slate rock westward of Lezant Point—close in shore, so near that her crew were taking in a cargo from the quarries worked in the precipitous face of the cliff—lay the French schooner in which Reine Helier had crossed the Channel. La Belle Marie floated easily in the deep dark water beneath the headland.

The last boat from the town had left her side,
laden with the freight imported from foreign
countries, and the skipper was busily engaged
in filling his vessel with the fine blue slate,
which was in great request abroad, and which
also afforded a pretext for a far more profitable
traffic. His dealings with the proprietors of
the slate-works had been fair and honourable.
Every load of the stone lowered into the
schooner was paid for before it touched the
deck. Many a trader from Holland or Nantes
was less scrupulous in his business transac-
tions than the smuggler, Jacob Mohr.

The mists of evening, which hung over
the frowning cliffs, and almost hid the
schooner, were dispelled in her Captain's
cabin by a brightly burning lamp which
swung in its centre. All the appurtenances
on which the light flashed, as it oscillated
with the slow heaving of the vessel while the
tide floated beneath her, were plain, but arranged with much neatness. The only ornaments were a few Flemish paintings arranged
against the bulkheads, in blackened frames of
ancient oak, mostly Madonnas. There was
little variety of subject, and they were treated
after the somewhat hard, cold, unimpassioned
manner of the early school to which they belonged; fair, frigid-looking women, more of
earth than heaven, with nothing beyond the

mother's love expressed in their unimaginative countenances.

In contrast with the devotional character of the pictures, the Dutchman's cabin was quaintly fitted up with articles which showed him to be, like most of his nation, a lover of order and comfort. Cups and basins of Nankin and Japanese ware, such as amateurs would delight to collect, and deep, richly-stained tumblers and beakers of Bohemian glass, hung from pegs, or were otherwise secured, so as to swing safely in a gale. Scriptural subjects again predominated in the designs presented by the tilings of the stove, taken chiefly from the history of the Saviour's birth. The stable at Bethlehem, the young Virgin Mother receiving the kings or the shepherds, were repeated in the white and blue porcelain. So constantly was the same idea recalled, that it seemed, if strange, not impossible, that even the name of the smuggler's vessel was chosen from some early, sacred association, not quite forgotten amidst the turmoil and hazard of his actual life.

The man at home in the state cabin of La Belle Marie—for nowhere else, it was said, but on board his vessel did Jacob Mohr willingly abide—was seated before his desk, and occupied in making an arithmetical calculation. Overhead, hurrying feet were passing to and fro—heavy burthens were being deposited on the deck. The tramp of men laden with her new cargo, mingled with the wash of the waves against the ship's sides, and the hoarse screaming of the gulls and puffins, which, disturbed from their nests in the crevices of the rocks, were circling angrily round the raking masts of the schooner. Jacob Mohr seemed satisfied that this vulgar labour was in good hands, and did not trouble himself farther than every now and then to raise his head and listen. When he had finished noting down the items of the transaction just completed, the Dutchman —as he was called by the sailors, though he professed to be a Hamburg trader—shut up the books, carefully wiped his pen, and placed it in its accustomed niche near that where the inkhorn was as securely deposited. His figure, as he rose from his stooping attitude, was taller than might have been supposed, and prevented his keeping quite erect as he passed under the beams. It was not stout, but firmly knit, with an appearance of vigorous strength in the well-turned limbs. His seaman's dress, neat in cut and texture, fitted loosely, so as to afford every joint and muscle free play. Not a tinge of grey mingled with the black locks, jetty as the walls of slate under which his vessel lay. The upper lip was smooth,

and the mouth, when closed, was firmly com-
pressed, and gave a marked expression of decision ·to the face, which was that of a man of
strong purposes and energetic resolution, advanced more than midway upon the journey
of life.

Perhaps the want of all affection and
pleasantness in his own home made Lance
Fleming—the only other person present—as
he watched the flickering lights reflected in
the porcelain walls of the stove, and petted
and played with his dog, lying stretched out
on the square of rich carpet at his feet, enjoy
the cheerful, well appointed cabin, and cordial
welcome of the foreigner. At all events, there
was something in his glance which caused the
features, contracted by the cares of business, to
relax, and Jacob Mohr said, good-humouredly,

"Come, you have been very patient. Let
us talk awhile. Bist ein braver Junker. Tell
me how you like the dog."

"Well enough; but he wants training.
At least, I have not the trick to manage him.
He runs too much after the petticoats."

"Ah!—so!—that is his fault? It is a
weakness which has ruined many great souls.
You must not be too hard upon my dog,"
said Mynheer, while a smile, which quite altered their expression, flitted over his features.
"He will do his work well, none the worse for

loving to follow the pretty maidens. There
was a young, handsome Haus-Frau where he
was reared; she gave him milk; he would
follow her to the world's end. If you
have women at your house who are kind to
him, out of love for you, he will follow them
as he did his old mistress. That is not a bad
trait."

"There are not many persons who will
take the trouble to be kind to any favourite
of mine, at Woods," said Lance, gloomily.
" It is not for my sake, but because she knew
him on board your vessel, that the French
girl you brought over from Brittany entices
him away from me. She speaks his language,
too ; the dog has no English. How am I to
make him understand what I want him to do,
when I do not know a word of his lingo?"

"Ha! Bouffe, old fellow, we are in a
difficulty!" said the Dutchman, pulling the
long ears of the spaniel, as it lay contentedly
on the carpet. " Why, you must get the
French girl to teach you, mot pour mot—see,
the dog pricks up its ears directly!—as she
read to you the Lieutenant's letter. Tausend
tonnen! you got through that dilemma ; and
here we are, thanks to her assistance, with the
vessel lightened of its cargo, and a lawful
freight on board, which may defy the scrutiny
of all the Revenue cruisers in Christendom."

Lance moved uneasily in his chair. "I don't think we behaved quite handsomely by her. Poor girl! how her eyes ran over when she saw that the cutter was to leave so soon! But it could not be helped. It would not suit us to have the Curlew in Lezant harbour, and her officer walking up and down before the gates at Woods, as if he were keeping the watch on board one of the King's men-of-war. Mr. Helier took him for a ghost. In the moonlight he had an eerie look; and, though we make a mock of such things when we are in gay company and broad sunshine, I can tell you it needs a bold spirit, and a clearer conscience than most of us possess, to stand the odd noises there, and face the queer spectres that come with the darkness; some real, some unreal—nothing but the wind, or the rats, or other things that shall be nameless; but now and then making the flesh of the bravest of us creep on his bones. Once, as you may have heard, there was a foul murder done there; and I've often thought, when I've been in my maddest humour, what would I do if my own father's spirit were to meet me face to face!"

Lance Fleming's voice dropped as he spoke, and his countenance became deadly pale. The skipper answered like a man who was a stranger to fear.

" Good ! — Suppose he did? For the most part, those who come from the grave visit us on no idle errand. These poor souls from the other world have some question to put or to answer ; and, if the fools would stop to listen or inquire, they might learn what would put an end to much sorrow. I have heard these ghosts at Woods accounted for. Some day we will go together, and see if they will dare to confront us ; the old Dutchman will not run away. Ah ! we will see into this matter presently."

" No, no ! best leave them alone," said Lance, sullenly. " I am not going to say whether I believe in them myself ; but there is not another person in the country-side but holds that Woods is haunted. Let it stay so."

" Aye, aye," said the foreigner ; " Lass es so stehen ! It is of no use troubling ourselves to alter what another day may suit us best just so. But, mark me, Junker ! *I* am no ghost. What makes Mr. Helier fear to have dealings in person with me ? I am very well pleased with you, but it is my custom to deal with principals. Half my cargo was consigned to the master at Woods. Why is he too proud to come on board my vessel ?"

" Mr. Helier is not the owner of Woods," answered Lance. " He is only Lord Boscawen's tenant, and is himself, as far as I know, a man without fortune or resources. Out of compassion, when my mother became a widow, she was allowed to continue on the farm, and then this man, who had been her husband's bailiff, managed the land for her. Two or three years afterwards she married him. I have been kept ignorant of most of the affairs of the family; but I am my father's only son, and consequently his heir. I believe Jean Helier tried to debase me, that I might not know my rights. Now I have shaken off my fetters, and made money. It was I who bought the goods. Helier has no dealings now with the free-traders."

"Sehr gut," said the cautious Dutchman. "Das ist recht!—that is all right. You are the principal, and will sign the release when the goods are safely delivered. I understand, and will make a note of it. But why has this man left off business? His name was in the books formerly."

"It may be so," said Lance, impatiently. "I know nothing of his early history. Sometimes I fancy it has been one marked with desperate crimes and stirring adventures. Now, he is a silent, moody man, frightened at his own shadow, crossed at times by starts of temper, prompting him to acts of violence. It is a trying thing to live with him."

The Dutchman strode across the cabin,

and opening a locker took out a thin, long-necked bottle, and two fine-stemmed glasses. He filled one for himself, and pushed the bottle over to Lance.

"Here is success to our venture, and may it not be the last! Never fear! it is strong, but it is pure. Your head will be the steadier for it, and I wish to drive these mists from your brains. I want to know more about this country, where, who knows, but I may lay my bones? unless, indeed, which I like better, the sea, which has been my home for many years, gives me a grave. I like these bold, black rocks, sinking down into the green waters. England suits me well. I shall sail away, but I shall come back again, and it will not be long first. Where shall our next landing be?"

"Here away!" said Lance, pointing down the long line of coast, but faintly visible through the cabin window in the mists of the falling night. "Beyond these bluffs there is a long stretch of sandy beach, overhung by lofty crags, from which it is dangerous, almost impossible to look. Men have met their death by venturing near them after dusk."

He paused abruptly. Mynheer took up his words quickly,—

"Yes, that was very unlucky! That was

the poor devil, what you call exciseman, who
wanted to spy out what was going on below."
I have heard of it from the sailors."

"No!" said Lance; "that was accident.
What I refer to was the work of design. The
man was walking near the edge of the cliff;
some say he had been drinking hard, but
this was contradicted in the evidence. There
was a trial, and no one could prove that he
was not in full possession of his senses. He
was walking, I say, close to the edge of that
mighty cliff, where it arches over the sea;
not alone, but in company with one who was
known to be his enemy—a rich man, who,
with plenty of flocks and herds of his own,
envied him his pet lamb. These two met in
anger, and but one was seen again in life;
the other was found—his mangled remains,
at least—lying dashed to fragments at the
base of the cliffs, six hundred feet below."

"That is not a pleasant tale, sapperment!
You are a gloomy nation," said the Dutchman, after a momentary pause; "and you
have cliffs and rocks that make a man's brain
turn only to stand upon them. It is better
in the even plains, by the willow-dykes of
Holland. But what for are you telling me
of this mischance, or murder?—though you
have not quite made it plain to me that the
man did not fall over for his own good will

and pleasure — I mean, by accident. What
has it to do with the landing of our next
cargo?"

"Only this, that the sands cannot well be
overlooked, and that boats might pull in from
a vessel without attracting observation," said
Lance. "We make even death and murder
serve our purposes, and learn to think but
little of the one or the other. You might run
the boats in upon the strand, and I will have
people ready to carry the goods into the
ravine. Once there, I will defy the Custom-
house officers to find them."

"I will take thought upon it," said the
skipper. "What if the cutter got wind of
our intentions? Though hid from eyes on
land, this shore you speak of may be watched
from the sea. I do not like to risk my precious vessel. You must get the French girl
to write a letter next time, and appoint her
lover to meet her up among the hills, far out
of our way."

The young man laughed. "That might
be managed," he said. "Now for a pull in
shore. Can you lend me a boat? My fellows, I will be bound for it, are drinking at
the Three Crowns."

They mounted together the short ladder
staircase leading to the deck. When they
reached it, the smuggler cast a quick glance

in the direction indicated by Lance as favourable for a landing.

"That is the extreme point where the
strand terminates," said Lance, in a whisper.
"It was from that beetling precipice that the
man of whom I was speaking fell, shot
through the body, or was cast down head-
long. You can see where the cliff looms out
into the fog, with the gulls circling round it.
When the corpse was found, hundreds of the
cormorants that haunt these cliffs were con-
gregated screaming over it."

He shuddered and turned his head away,
but the Dutchman kept his eyes fixed on the
distant cliff, while he asked several questions
respecting the state of tide and wind when it
was safest to approach the shore, and the return he was to expect for his cargo;—all of
the most practical kind. Then, with a sudden
change of manner, he said in an abrupt, decided tone,—

"That is England! I have not set foot
on your soil since I was first engaged in these
matters. It will be dark night soon. Let us
go ashore together."

He ordered a boat to be lowered, and
they were soon, with the mate and one other
sailor, pulling in the direction of the ravine
below the old house at Woods.

The men knew the skipper's humour, and

bent silently over their oars. Impelled by
four strong arms, the boat rose and fell rapidly over the long swells of the billows,
which in the calmest weather beat upon that
coast. Nevertheless, as Mynheer had fore-
told, it was dark when they reached the
shore.

Not a word was spoken among the party
as they made fast the boat, and leaving the
seaman in charge of her, the skipper and the
mate, with Lance Fleming, plunged at once
into the deep shadow of the woods that
fringed the banks of the stream, bending
over it so closely that only here and there a
stray gleam from the moon, which was rising
over the sea, was caught and reflected back
from the surface of the water. Lance went
first to show the way, followed by Mynheer;
the mate bringing up the rear.

As they passed the Keeve, Lance pointed
out to the captain of the French vessel marks
in the stone walls, known to few, which showed
where the rock was hollowed out in cavities,
filled at present with valuable contraband
goods landed from the schooner. Mohr, however, scarcely seemed like the same steady-
going, serious trader, who had superintended
with so much vigilance the shipment of the
heavy freight of slate which had replaced her
late cargo on board the smuggling vessel.

"Forward!" he said, impatiently. "The goods are safe : I have washed my hands of them. See you to that. Now, let us go to your old house. It cannot be far off."

Lance pushed his way through the pathless labyrinth, parting the boughs with main strength. The crashing sound guided the men who followed him, for in the wood it was pitch dark ; they could see nothing.

"Himmel und Hölle! Have you wild beasts in these dens and caves?" said the Dutchman, as they stopped for a moment to gain breath after a sharp ascent. "This is more like an Indian jungle—a Hottentot bush country—than an English wood. How much more of it is there?"

"We are almost through the worst," said Lance. "My mother's house is not half-a-mile off, but there is a tough conflict with the boughs yet to come before we reach it. You see, it is a capital hiding-place."

"Aye, aye!" said the mate. "The tubs are safe enough. I only wish we had brought more with us: but it was ticklish weather, and it doesn't do to draw much water if you want to creep along the coast unseen. Is that you, Bouffe? what's afoot beside ourselves this dark night? The dog scents something."

The men stood still, looking through the thin screen of brushwood, which now alone intervened between them and the neglected pleasure-grounds belonging to the old Manor-house. In the avenue which traversed the domain they could hear the tread of a slow, uncertain footstep.

"That is Mr. Helier!" said Lance, in a whisper. "He often walks late, but a slight thing frightens and drives him in. There is no occasion for us to cross his path."

He would have drawn back, with the intention of following a different track, but Mynheer impatiently shook off his detaining hand, and stepped forward into the avenue, just where a white gush of moonlight streamed through the trees. Either he disregarded the presence of the timid master of Woods, or he calculated on Lance's hint that he was easily terrified. In the shadowy glimmering of the moon-lighted avenue, Mohr's form seemed to grow taller. It would have needed less than that sudden apparition to scare the unhappy being, who, from eve till daybreak, was the sport of superstitious terrors. For one instant he stood still, spell-bound; then, with a wild cry for aid, he fled towards the house.

"That is the way!" said his step-son, laughing. "You see, he is an arrant coward. We shall not be troubled with him to-night. You have frightened him half out of his senses."

"That is my good friend, Mr. Helier of Woods," said the Dutchman, composedly. "I thought I was right. His name is in my books. We have certainly had dealings together."

"He did not seem inclined to stop for conversation," said Lance, still laughing. "A groan — anything, nothing — suffices to drive him indoors. There was no need to show yourself."

"Did he take me for the ghost?" said Mohr. "Ah, that is pleasant — that is just as it should be! I do not think we should be very good company, this Mr. Helier of Woods, and I. Now, I can always get rid of him."

"Nothing can be easier," answered Lance. "There are parts of his own house in which he has not set foot for years. A more abject trembler does not breathe."

"Put me there!" said the Dutchman, phlegmatically. "I will sleep in the bed, I will breathe the air of the room which he disaffects so much. Mind, I am not timid! I will sleep in that pleasant ghost-chamber at Woods this very night. If there is anything in those old stories, I should like to know the truth. We will sift the matter thoroughly."

"You shall have it your own way," said Lance, gravely. "All of us are not cowards,

like Jean Helier; yet few, if any, would take
your place. Now, come on; the coast is
clear. Yonder is the house, and it is as dark
and silent as the grave."

They crossed the courtyard, which was
lighted only by the moon, and entered the
cheerless-looking mansion by a side-door, the
key of which was in Lance's possession.

Mynheer gazed about him curiously, as,
after striking a light, Lance guided him
through the dim passages of Lord Boscawen's
Grange. Not a door—not a figure on the
tapestry—not one of the mouldy old family
pictures—escaped his notice.

"Schlaf und Tod!" he said, at last.
"Yours is a quiet house, Herr Fleming!
Nothing stirs—yes, what have we here?—
Einen Frauen-Zimmer!—I will wager my life
something younger than the housekeeper you
told me of wakes or sleeps behind this closed
door."

He stopped abruptly, as Bouffe had done,
at an angle in the obscure passage.

"Yes, that is Mademoiselle Helier's chamber. "She has quick ears, and does not go
to bed so early as the rest," said Lance, under
his breath. "Let us pass on. She has a
quiet conscience. We shall not frighten her
easily."

"I do not wish to terrify her—Fraulein

Reine!"—said the skipper, still lingering near the door. " A pious, good Mädchen, who said her prayers and sang her hymns when she sailed with us! What should she fear? Might one not say good night? We were compagnons de voyage."

" No, no!—come on! What are you waiting for?" said Lance, impatiently. " Mademoiselle Reine is, no doubt, asleep. We saw no light on this side of the house when we were below."

" She has struck a match since we have been standing here," said Mynheer, pointing to a faint gleam which came from under the door. " Ah, her senses are very quick; she is French; vive, alerte!—a mouse could not stir without waking her. She is listening now!"

" So much the more reason for our moving on," said Lance. " The French girl is not on our side. She corresponds with the new Revenue officer. Probably, she is betrothed to him. Richard Osborne will have an active spy in our house, if she is as quick of ear and eye as you say."

Jacob Mohr turned away from the young girl's door as Lance spoke. " Ah, you do not know. Who can tell the secrets of a woman's heart?" he said, somewhat sentimentally. " Kann seyn, oder kann nicht seyn. We shall see."

· They had left by this time the gallery into which Reine's chamber opened, and entered another of the winding passages that abounded in the old house. It was full of odd steps, and shelves, and crannies; and in the thick walls there were strangely-shaped recesses; one of which Lance pointed out to Mynheer as the spot where tradition affirmed that a child's coffin had been immured, the form of the little walled-up niche having doubtless given rise to the idea.

"These are your quarters, Mynheer," said Lance, opening a door at the end of the passage. "If your courage fails, I can put you elsewhere. The room is not usually occupied; but Mr. St. Erme, the clergyman at Lezant, slept here a month ago: or, rather, kept watch, for the ghosts he professed to lay are said to have given him an uneasy night. This is the haunted chamber."

They entered, as Lance spoke, a large, well-proportioned room, full of ancient furniture, and, consequently, more comfortable in aspect than most of the upper chambers at Woods. Wardrobes and cabinets, which creaked and groaned so as to annoy Mr. Helier's sensitive nerves, had been banished thither, and several dark old pictures, on which he did not care to look, hung on the walls. By daylight, it might be seen that in each of

these there was something of a repulsive nature; but, at present, only their handsome
frames caught the eye. Mohr crossed the
floor, and gazed with strong interest round
him, at the velvet-canopied couch, the quaint
ebony cabinets and toilet ornaments, and.
the one gem of Italian art hanging over the
mantel-piece—a copy, probably, of one of
Raphael's matchless Madonnas.

"Heilige Mutter Gottes!" he said, doffing
his cap, as he stood contemplating the picture, with his arms folded tightly across his
chest. "I should not fear to sleep on the
verge of the bottomless pit, with those saint-
like eyes watching over me! Nothing evil will
come near me to-night."

"Well, I think I can insure you against
living men, and, if your conscience is clear,
you are probably safe from ghostly terrors,"
said Lance. "Mine has often reproached me
for many a boyish, practical joke played off
on my stepfather and Leah, as well as for
more mischievous stratagems to keep the
enemy from prying into our hiding-places.
But you are one of ourselves, and too sharp-
sighted to be taken in by the flash of an old
magic lantern on the wall, and the music of
Madame Fleming's Eolian harp. Though I
can account for a good many odd sights and
sounds, there are some, I can assure you,
about this old house, which baffle me."

Mohr answered, in his usual half-serious manner,—

"I do not think I shall be afraid to rest my head where your good parish-priest passed the night; though there have been deeds done in some of these old places fit to make men shudder, and even to rouse the dead—worse than the tale of bloodshed and murder you told me in my cabin. Men should not jest in such a house as this."

He shook off impatiently the hand Lance laid on his arm, as the youth tried to draw him away to another apartment, where refreshments were laid out. When he was alone, Mohr resumed his contemplation of the picture; and, free from observation, his countenance bore marks of strong emotion. There were tears in the eyes of the man, usually self-possessed and stern, or at times full of a sort of· reckless gaiety—as he stood, with his cap thrown off, gazing at that youthful, saint-like face. After the manner of the great master, the Holy Virgin was pourtrayed as a calm, fair maiden, with hands meekly folded, while, above her soft, light hair, a golden glory was faintly indicated.

The skipper of La Belle Marie walked slowly up and down the chamber, noting all its contents. He took from a stand, where it had reposed for years, an old repeating watch; and, after examining the works, which were quite uninjured by time, wound it up carefully, making it strike the hour. Its clear bell-like tone carried his thoughts back to a far-distant time, and increased the gloom which had gathered over him since he entered the old house.

Fleming's murder, or, at least, circumstances connected with that event, became, under the dismal influence of the locality, strongly borne in upon his mind. In another hemisphere, he had heard the story from lips now silent, which had revealed to him other details than those Lance had communicated, and such, too, as were capable of a very different construction.

As Mohr pondered over all he knew and suspected in that haunted room, sleep became an impossibility; the hours of the night appeared too precious to be wasted; and trimming the hand-lamp Lance had set down, the smuggling captain left the chamber, and following the light sound of footsteps down the passage, found his way without difficulty to the part of the house occupied by Jean Helier and his family.

CHAPTER VIII.

THE hours of that night had worn very slowly away to the occupants of the small room over the principal entrance, whence, on her first arrival at Woods, Reine saw a pale face looking down. This apartment, which was not a sleeping chamber, belonged particularly to the master of the house: not that he was partial to solitude, for no one could dislike being alone more than Mr. Helier. His unhappy, sickly wife, kept him company in his long vigils, if other society was unattainable; and daylight often broke upon them before their eyes had closed in slumber: though they were, neither of them, strong persons, and the woman's shrunken form was bowed down, and her senses, never acute, were chilled and dulled by fatigue and want of rest.

On this occasion, Reine Helier enlivened the gloomy couple by passing constantly in and out of the scantily-furnished and dimly-lighted chamber, at the top of the broad oak staircase in the centre of the building, where they were sitting up, long after the inmates of most English farm-houses would be in their beds. Mr. Helier had come in-doors at ten o'clock, white and faint, shuddering with aguish cold; and the goodnatured French girl had offered to make him some warm, comfortable *tisane*, which might bring the life back to his chilled frame. He had accepted her offer readily, and the narrow but lofty room looked more cheerful than usual, with the fire Reine had lighted burning brightly in the grate, and the rug she had dragged in from one of the disused parlours laid down before the ancient, sculptured chimneypiece. Her cousin was sitting at one corner, sipping the fragrant beverage she had distilled for him from herbs; on the opposite side of the hearth stood a large empty arm-chair, which Reine had placed there for his wife.

Mrs. Helier, however, had preferred to sit away from the fire, in a distant part of the room. Her figure could only be dimly discerned when she lifted herself up from the attitude of hopeless dejection into which she had sunk. Hour after hour passed away unheeded; and neither the husband nor the wife proposed to go to rest. Mr. Helier sat dozing by the burning logs; while the wretched partner of his life swayed herself

backwards and forwards as was her wont,
disturbing him sometimes from his dreamy
tranquillity, which never amounted to sleep,
by the grating on the oak boards of the legs
of her chair, when she moved it incautiously
quicker than usual.

On the table lay Reine's neat work, with
a candle beside it. There was no other light
save that cast by the flickering flames. Something more nearly approaching to a smile than
ordinary stirred the muscles of Mr. Helier's
face when she came back, having been away
for some time, and sat down quietly to her
occupation, after inquiring if he felt better.
He had thought that she was gone to rest,
and had left him with only that wearisome
companion, who was rocking herself dismally
in the back-ground. Though he hated it, he
fancied at times that absolute solitude would
have been preferable to her company.

Reine's voice, speaking the accents of his
never-forgotten native province — the well-re-
membered scent of the warm drink she had
prepared for him — the outline of her features,
which resembled the lineaments of sisters and
brothers of whom he had seen nothing for
years, comforted the lonely, broken-spirited
man, and warmed his heart. He liked to see
his young kinswoman, so full of life and animation, with her pleasant French manners

and neat appearance, sitting near him and attending to his wants.

Reine was proceeding silently with her work, when, as if coming from a remote part of the house, a very distinct sound of footsteps was heard in the passage. Mr. Helier dropped the spoon with which he was stirring his tisane, and sank back in his chair; while his wife ceased rocking, and leaned forward in hers, peering with dim eyes out of the gloom. The steps, meanwhile, came on, and stopped at the room-door, of which the handle was turned unhesitatingly.

In that haunted house, at the dead of night, for the clock was on the stroke of twelve — when the servants were long since gone to rest, and the outer doors bolted and barred, it was certainly somewhat startling to hear that measured tread upon the passage-floor. Still, if Mr. and Mrs. Helier had possessed stronger nerves, it might have struck them that there was nothing ghost-like in the sound. It was a man's foot, firmly planted, which was heard so audibly in the corridor.

Reine had gone on with her work, without showing any sign of terror. Perhaps the step was familiar to her ear, for the colour rose bright and warm to her face while she listened to it. There might, on stormy nights, have

been comfort in the sound of that regular footfall overhead, as she lay awake in the little
state-cabin of the smuggling schooner.   As
the door opened, she looked up brightly;
while Mr. Helier's head sank on his hands,
and a faint gasping sigh burst from his wife's
lips — the first utterance that had passed them
since nightfall.   Reine welcomed the intruder
with a blush and a smile.

Mynheer came forward quickly.   There
was nothing ghost-like in his figure, and he
too smiled when his eyes met Reine's beaming
glance.

"It is Captain Mohr," she said, anxious
to re-assure the trembling couple; "the kind
friend who brought me over from Brittany.
He knows all our people.   Cousin, will you
not bid him welcome?"

Mr. Helier recovered himself slowly.   It
took him several moments to shake off the
deadly fear which had assailed him.   Meanwhile, all was dark and silent at the other
end of the room.   The monotonous sound of
the rocking had quite ceased, and Mrs.
Helier's form was invisible, as she lay sunk
back, with her head resting against the high
carved framework of her chair.   The smuggler
did not at first speak to either of them, but
remained at the table conversing in a low
tone with Reine; then, at her invitation, he

took the vacant chair near her, and beside the hearth.

The master of the house roused himself to look at him. As he gazed fixedly at the sailor-like, powerfully-knit form opposite to him, with the firelight glancing on the dark handsome face, and glittering in the bold eyes of the stranger, his courage returned, and he said, with more self-possession and courtesy than might have been expected from him,—

"We are your debtors, Captain Mohr, for bringing this good girl among us. See, she has been nursing me to-night. To what do I owe the pleasure of this unexpected visit? Reine! Monsieur wishes to drink your health. Apportez du vin!"

"Do not stir, Mademoiselle!" said Mynheer, laying his hand on her arm. "I have done that already, each night since you honoured my vessel by accepting a passage in her to England. La Belle Marie is off the coast now. When your visit is ended, you can have your cabin. Say, shall it be so?"

The smuggling Captain cast a glance round the chamber, and into the dim recess whence now and then a sigh might he heard. Very possibly he repented having brought the pretty maiden from "la belle France" to such a gloomy place.

"No, no!" said Mr. Helier, in an agitated tone. " I cannot part with Reine. She has made herself necessary to us. Was that your business here ?"

"Not entirely," said the foreigner. "Mademoiselle has but to speak the word, however, and I am at her service. I am glad she has made friends already. Herr Fleming brought me with him from my vessel. He is gone to his rest now, and it is best he should know nothing of this meeting. Now, to business. My visit to him was made under a false impression. The name of Helier deceived me. It is on our books, and now I find — the Junker tells me — that you have given up taking any part in our ventures. Why is this? Has there been any failure on our part, or have you so much wealth that the gold burns your fingers? Let us understand each other."

A deep flush mounted to the cheeks which a few moments before had been ghastly white, as Mr. Helier heard the smuggling Captain's question.

"Is the name on the books still?" he answered. " I thought my old friends had forgotten me."

"Ach, not so! We have longer memories than you think for," said Mohr. " Tausend tonnen! I am young — what you call junior

—in the firm myself; but I have looked into
these matters deeply. Your people are my
colleagues; and I could tell you, going back
into the past, things that would astonish you,
and make your blood circulate more quick
than it seems to do now. Those were brisk
days when you and poor Gervase Helier kept
the Revenue-lads on the look-out, night after
night, and seldom failed to run a cargo ashore.
Brisk days, I say! and they seem to have
answered well with you, mein freund, since
you live in a house fit for a lord, while he ——
ach wohl!—I saw him not long after—it had
fared ill with your old comrade. Bah! we
will not talk of that now. I am glad to see
you in better spirits. I only spoke of those
times to show you that the French Brothers
are still remembered among us."

"Merci!" said Helier, drawing a long
breath, as if recovering from deadly terror.
"Gervase is not in good odour here. Say no
more about him. He once put forward an
imprudent claim, which Lord Boscawen has
never forgiven. It might cost me his favour,
and my present comfortable position, if our old
connexion were mentioned. Still he was
mon frère bien aimé!—your father's cousin,
Reine. When did Mynheer last see him?"

"Several years ago," said Mohr, significantly. "He had another name, then;
but he still answered more readily to the old

one. Our house has correspondents in all
those distant islands. Even now our ware-
houses are full, and I have brought with me
to St. Malo a rich cargo. Not such goods as
Herr Fleming has taken off my hands ; but
excellent cigars, spices, and coffee. I have
the samples with me. The bulk of the
goods are in safe hiding. I shall run across
with them the first dark night after I get
back to France."

He drew out from the capacious pocket of
his rough coat, as he spoke, a packet which he
handed over to Mr. Helier, who examined it
with the air of a connoisseur in such matters.

" Ah, they are real Havannahs ! I brought
them myself from Cuba," said Mohr, as the
man opposite to him, animated and interested,
unfolded the papers in which the cigars were
wrapped. " Try one, you will not be disappointed. Unless, indeed," he added, with
instinctive politeness scarcely to be expected
from one of his calling, " the odour is dis-
pleasing to these ladies."

It seemed strange that he should have
discovered the presence of the silent woman
at the far end of the chamber ; but perhaps
the eyes which had avoided the bright light of
the lamp in his own cabin, were stronger in
the dark old chamber at Woods.

" That does not signify," said Helier,
roughly. " Reine does not mind it, I will be

bound. But I am no smoker; I cannot bear it. My head is not strong."

Mynheer lighted one of the cigars, and the sweet perfume of the choice Indian weed stole on the air.

"In my country," he said, "die Frauen have their cigarettes, too. I mean," he added, correcting himself, "in the lands where I have lived long — the Moluccas — beyond seas, in short — Dutch, Spanish — it is all much the same to me. I am one citizen of the world."

He puffed away gravely, speaking at intervals, while the cloud diffused around him partially obscured his features. Reine, meanwhile, had risen, and, after trimming the fire and candle, was preparing to depart.

"Do not go, Fraulein! I will throw the cigar into the fire if it displeases you. See, I am a foreigner — I do not quite understand your customs. Of all the countries of the globe, though I can speak her language, England is the strangest. Ach! we may live years, and not see through the mists which hang round this little island! Stay, Mademoiselle! I want to set this small matter of business plain before Mr. Helier. I will, if he likes it, give him a chance to make a fortune. It is on the cards, if he will play one hand right. Shall I go on?"

"Yes," said Helier; "I have felt more alive to-night than I have been for years. The old times come over me. Ah, those were merry days! I am sorry Gervase paid such a price for them. I am not sure that I came off better; only my punishment has been slower. Assez, assez!" he added, impatiently, as if rebuking himself for adverting to his own unhappy state of mind. "What were you going to say to me?"

"Only to propose that the next cargo should be, in fact, consigned to you, as the last was in name. Herr Fleming has not chosen to give us his own. I do not quite like such reservations. Here is the invoice— is not that what you call it? Will it suit you to join us in this transaction?"

Helier took the paper eagerly. His eye ran quickly down the long list of goods.

"Yours is the very place to run such a cargo aground; yonder, on the beach where I landed with the Junker, under the great headland which has the good old British King's name. No one likes to go round it after dark. There are bad tales afloat; and, like this old house where you live, which seems to me right warm and pleasant, the shores of the creek in the woods are said to be haunted. There was a man murdered there—pushed off the cliff—years ago."

" Stop !" said Helier, while a deep sound like weeping came from the end of the chamber.

" It was her husband," he added, in a whisper, leaning across the fireplace, and pointing cautiously towards his wife. " Do not speak on that subject."

" Recht wohl !" said the foreigner. " It makes no odds. The place has a bad name — that is all I will say — and suits our purpose. Give me your hand upon the bargain. You shàll have the risk and the profits, and you will find that Jacob Mohr will not cheat you. Are you satisfied ? "

He extended a brown, but well-formed hand, to Mr. Helier, who slightly touched it. The smuggler's grasp was firm as iron.

" Give us pens and ink, Mademoiselle," said Mohr, reseating himself, as if not quite pleased with his new colleague's manner. " We will have it down in writing. I am, above all things, a man of business, and like to know what I have to trust to."

He drew up, in a stiff, foreign-looking hand, an agreement, which he passed over to Mr. Helier, who read it through carefully.

" I can find no objection to your terms," he said. " All is fair and honourable. But we must have a witness."

" Here is Mademoiselle," said the smuggler, affixing his own signature, and then handing the paper to Mr. Helier. " I shall like to see her pretty writing, and she will not betray us."

" Do not depend upon that !" said Reine, her cheeks glowing, her eyes glittering. " I will not put my name to that paper. You must find another witness."

Mr. Helier looked at her with surprise. The smuggling Captain's glance was very penetrating.

" She is extremely perverse !" her cousin said, at last. " I think it is of no use to argue with her; and, besides, she is too young. What must we do ? It would be ill-advised to admit any one else into our counsels."

" Well, we must trust each other," said the smuggler. " It is no matter about witnesses, since our affair is not one concerning which we can go to law. Only I thought I should like to have Mademoiselle's name at the bottom of the paper. Now, I must bid you good-night. It will soon be time for the fowls — what you call cock-crow ! I must sleep."

Mr. Helier looked perplexed.

" We have seldom a guest here. The rooms are not prepared, but we will do our best. Where can you put Mynheer ?"

He did not appeal to his silent wife, but looked at Reine.

"Ah, I have a capital Schlafzimmer! I am happy as a king with the Heilige Jungfrau smiling upon me from the wall, and the sea, that I so love, sounding at a distance. I have the best room in your old house, my good friend! but it has not been often slept in lately, I fancy. Still, it is not cold or damp, and I prefer it."

"Does he mean the room that Mr. St. Erme occupied last?" Mr. Helier said, turning pale. "Anywhere but there—any other would be better. See to it, Reine!"

"I like my room : there is nothing wrong about it," said the foreigner, rising. "Mademoiselle, perhaps, will have the goodness to show me the way; for it is far off, and I lost myself more than once in coming here. I do not think I should find it again."

Reine lighted a small hand-lamp, which she had brought with her from France, and rose to accompany the stranger. Mr. Helier had sunk back into his arm-chair, and hardly noticed his departure. His wife neither spoke nor stirred.

"That is dull company!" said the skipper, as the door closed behind them. "My child, I do not like to leave you here. I will not ask you to go with me now, because the cutter is looking out for us, and you might be frightened. I shall not let the Lieutenant set foot on my deck. He will be back to-morrow, and we must make a quick passage across the Channel. Shall I come again, and fetch you away from these strange, grim beings? You are like an angel among demons."

"No, merci!" said Reine, who had listened attentively. "Never mind me. This man is of my own kindred, and will protect me. Like yourself, I have no fears."

The smuggler looked at her with strong admiration.

"That is the spirit I love!" he said. "Honest and true, tender and cheerful! I wish there were more like you in the world. But be advised. That scowling man is not trustworthy. Let me carry you back to France!"

"Leben Sie wohl!" said Reine, putting the light in his hand, and laughing, as she used one of the few expressions in his own language, which she had caught during her passage in the schooner. "That is the door of your chamber. I can find my way in the dark."

Then, in spite of an effort on his part to detain her, she flitted along the gloomy passages of the haunted house, unappalled by ghostly terrors, and found her way back safely to her own sleeping chamber.

CHAPTER IX.

RICHARD OSBORNE, deceived by false information, had spent two days looking out for the
schooner at the entrance of the Bristol Channel, and searching every creek among the
dreary, contorted rocks of the carboniferous
formation, with ribbon-like bands of rusty
slate, which meet the rolling waves where
the narrower sea opens off Hartland Point
to the broad Atlantic. Not a trace of La
Belle Marie, or her rich freight, had rewarded
him for his exertions.

He was furious at the disappointment,
especially when intelligence reached him from
a more trustworthy source that the landing
his heart was set upon interrupting, was intended to take place at the very spot he had
so lately quitted. The wind was not in his favour, and it would take more time than suited
his impatience for the Curlew to beat up
against it along the coast. Having laid his
plans carefully, he profited by the quickest
conveyances then procurable, and found him-

self, after a hurried journey, set down a few miles from Lezant, alone, and meaning to enter the town on foot, on the side farthest from the sea.

The undulating surface of the downs lay round him, dark and quiet. Those great, green sheep-pastures, with, at intervals, a track crossing them, or hollows filled with trees and imprisoned waterfalls, were always inexpressibly lonely. A few stars twinkled faintly aloft, and no moon was visible. It was a great contrast to the darkness and solitude in which Osborne had been moving for the last two hours, when the lights of Lezant town came in sight. Every house on the naps, as he approached the place, seemed to be illuminated; and persons, intent on business or pleasure, were rushing up and down the street. The Three Crowns was in a perfect blaze: the red gleam, from fire and candle, shining across the road. Higher up, on the rising ground before the inn, where Reine had stood to see the Curlew sail away, a crowd of people were assembled. The young officer remained for some time on the dark hill-side above, watching their proceedings, and then turned down a back lane, leading, by a circuitous route, to the quay.

As he walked on, with his hat pulled over his brows, and his rough coat, underneath which a brace of loaded pistols was concealed, buttoned up to his chin, Richard Osborne knew well that he would have paid the forfeit of discovery with his life. There were dozens of people, not twenty yards from him, who would have thought little, under such circumstances, of murder; but the throng in the public street was too much taken up with the night's work to heed the solitary foot-passenger, who stopped repeatedly, in spite of the danger he was incurring, whenever the irregular openings between the houses allowed him a glimpse of what was going forward.

In quite another direction, a solitary spark shone out from amidst the Parsonage evergreens. It was the gleam of the lamp which always burned so late in the Rector's study. Richard had seen it as he crossed the down, even before the windings of the hills brought the lights of the town into view; and with it there had come upon him the recollection of the white-haired, feeble man, to whom darkness had been intolerable since his futile attempt to exorcise the ghost at Woods had subjected his weakened mind to the most fearful visitations.

The by-way he had been threading, in almost total darkness, brought Richard Osborne out into the road at the bottom of the street of Lezant. He had not encountered one human being; and crossing the main causeway, he hurried on, still unobserved, along a foot-track, equally solitary, conducting to the back-gate of the premises belonging to the Boscawen Arms, which was shut up, and, as it had been from an early hour in the evening, entirely dark and still. Nevertheless, when the Lieutenant knocked at the kitchen-passage door, it was opened to him immediately by Morgan Price himself.

"All right, Sir!" he said, without any manifestation of surprise at seeing Osborne: "I guessed you might think it right to come back, and sat up for you. Come in at once. Now that you know something of Lezant hill-folk, I need hardly say that you run a great risk."

"No matter," said the young officer, as he stepped within the passage, while Price fastened the door. "I shall be careful; but these fellows will not find it easy to gull me again. Just let me have a light in my old sitting-room. I must ask you, late as it is, to sit up a little longer, or to lend me a latch-key. There are lights in Mr. St. Erme's house. He is a magistrate, is he not? and therefore bound to assist us. There is no time to be lost; and I mean to see him, if possible, before I sleep."

"Best not, Sir: leave it till morning," said

the landlord, earnestly. " The people will be separating soon, and you might meet some of them straggling home. I would not advise you to go out again."

The Lieutenant paid no attention to his warning, but, taking the light from his hand, went into the parlour which he had previously occupied, and busied himself for a few minutes in writing at the table. His face, through its extreme gravity, looked older than it had done when he first came to Lezant; and the cloud had not cleared off when he rose, and telling Price that he should not be away more than half-an-hour, left the house, which was shut up again instantly.

Though he had seemed in haste, Richard Osborne walked slowly along the path by which, once before, Morgan Price's child had conducted him to the church, which was close to Mr. St. Erme's dwelling. Perhaps the slowness of his pace, and his apparent in-attention to surrounding objects, prevented his being much noticed; for one or two persons passed him on the way, but they did not stop to look at him. His dress, though that of a gentleman, was plain, and partially dis-guised him. It was not at all like the careless sailor's garb in which he had so often taken his way through the street of Lezant. The darkness also befriended him.

He was so wrapped in thought that he passed the gate into the churchyard, and had to retrace his steps. Then, however, he roused himself, when conscious of his mistake, and his manner became firm and resolute. He opened the small gate into Mr. St. Erme's grounds, which was merely on the latch, and, following the windings of the gravel-path leading from the church, came to a glass-door close to the window, within which the light was still burning. After searching for some minutes he found a bell, which he pulled gently, but decidedly, and waited the result.

Every one in the house, except its master, was at rest. Never, at such an hour, were the inmates of the Parsonage disturbed. It was true that in Lezant, as in other places, sharp attacks of illness, strokes of death, came to manhood, old age, and infancy, at all hours and at unexpected seasons; but no one thought, on such occasions, of troubling the parson. Children went to their graves unbaptized—old men dropped off to their last repose, without its occurring to any one that it was proper to send at midnight for the pastor who had for so long a time allowed his flock to go astray in the wilderness, satisfied with summoning them together at stated intervals, and visiting them only when compelled by custom in the regular exercise of his vocation.

This careless shepherd, nevertheless, was awake, with all his senses in activity, when Richard Osborne's summons broke upon his vigils. So many sounds rang in his ear at midnight — voices and steps, appeals and threatenings, for which he could find no natural cause — that he did not at first know whether the sounds were real or fancied. The next minute the bell was pulled a second time, louder than before.

The Minister of Lezant was no coward. He put aside his books, and, without a moment's hesitation, stepped into the passage, and opened the glass-door into his garden, which was never fastened till he retired to rest. Very often he paced the walks of his quiet territory half the night through, and this mode of egress was left open for him.

Richard Osborne was standing in the dark porch covered with honeysuckle, which was emitting its fragrance in the night air. His tall figure was all that could be distinguished.

"There is no one but myself stirring in the house," Mr. St. Erme said. "What is your business with me? Can it not wait till morning?"

"Not if you can listen to me now, Mr. St. Erme," said Richard, baring his head respectfully to the grey-haired clergyman. "I

have undertaken an important duty, in which
you can aid me. You are a magistrate for
this county?"

Mr. St. Erme had stepped back, as if relieved
from any apprehension he might have entertained respecting the character of his visitor,
when the gentlemanlike accent of the young
officer fell on his ear. "You are come, then,"
he said, " on justice business? On that plea,
I invite you to enter."

He walked slowly into the study, as he
spoke, followed by Lieutenant Osborne.

As the light of the lamp shone upon the
frank, fair face, not untroubled by emotion, of
his guest, Mr. St. Erme became calmer and
colder. Osborne, on the contrary, was very
visibly agitated.

" Take time, Sir!" said Mr. St. Erme,
politely pointing to a seat. " You have perhaps hurried yourself in walking here. It is
late, but my occupations are not important.
Explain yourself at your leisure."

There was something so phlegmatic in his
air, that Osborne thrust down the emotion
which at first threatened to overpower him.
After a momentary pause, he said,—

" I will, then, open the business on which
I came to you without any preamble. You
are, I think, aware that I am an officer of His
Majesty's navy, at present in command of a

Revenue vessel off this coast. What else concerns me is of no consequence : we will, therefore, not touch upon it," he observed, speaking quickly and bitterly. " You can, if you doubt any of my assertions, examine these documents. A very valuable cargo of contraband articles has been landed to-night on Lezant quay. Part of this property has been concealed on the premises belonging to the inn called the Three Crowns, in the upper village. I wish to have a warrant to search for it."

Mr. St. Erme had taken up and carefully perused the papers handed over to him by the Lieutenant.

" That is enough," he said, giving them back. " It is extremely probable that your impression is correct. Do you wish me to accompany you on your errand to-morrow? There may, perhaps, be some disturbance. Lezant is an unruly place."

Osborne looked with respect at the fragile but venerable form of the clergyman.

" I should be sorry to ask you to take any step which might involve disagreeable consequences. No doubt, your presence would impart to us additional authority ; but I am fully prepared to meet any odds the people of Lezant can bring against me. They will be taken by surprise completely. Half the crew

of my cutter will be here to-morrow; and I
have written to the officer at the head of the
Customs at Camelford to come over with an
additional force to support me. I do not
apprehend any serious resistance."

"No doubt you are right," said Mr. St.
Erme. "Still, my support of the constituted
authorities has never been withheld. I shall
be with you in good time. You are at the
Boscawen Arms?"

"Yes," said Richard, struggling with
feelings which he controlled with difficulty.
"It is the only house in Lezant which, without your authorisation, I can enter. In a
place like this, though, notwithstanding a
foreign education, all my affections are
English, I am compelled to lead the life of an
alien."

He looked round as he spoke. Truly, in
that ascetic man's study, there were but small
indications of comfort; yet, in the searching,
melancholy glance which now surveyed it,
there was a yearning for those domestic ties
which the name and appearance of a home
suggest to one whose life is passed on the
turbulent waves.

Mr. St. Erme scarcely seemed to notice
the remark. "Now, I must bid you good
night," he said. "There is the warrant. I
am sorry that it is not in my power to offer

you any refreshment; but my niece and all
my domestics are gone to their beds."

He rose, and let Richard out into the
night air, as he spoke. They did not shake
hands, but parted, as they had met, like
strangers. Reginald St. Erme, however,
watched with a pang at his heart the tall figure
receding slowly along the gravel-walk.

As usual, after a night of riotous uproar,
Lezant was profoundly quiet the next morning,
until it began to be whispered abroad that
there were several strangers in the place.
The Lieutenant had not shown himself; but
from Camelford some of the Revenue police
had come down, and persons who were about
early had recognised two or three of the
seamen of the cutter.

Suspicion was kindled, and flew like wildfire up the street; and a larger party than
usual met in the tap-room of the Three
Crowns, where Mrs. Brock and Andrew
ministered liberàlly to their entertainment.

What's in the wind now, Dame?" said
one of the most frequent customers at the old
inn. "Hast heard the news? I can make
nought of it. What's brought the Excise
lads to our town? Why, it's half full of
sailors. Is there mischief afoot?"

"Like enough," said the Dame, grimly.
"I told you last night you were not half

careful. A fool and his money's soon parted, and some of you seem not to know how to make noise enough, when you're brawling in the streets. Now, what's said here between four walls, I'll engage goes no further."

"Let 'em come!" said Andrew, who had by no means recovered from his excesses the night before. "Why shouldn't they, when all 's safe?—aye, just as snug as the dead bodies in the churchyard. But, I say, just look ye, mother! if there isn't our old Passon! What's brought him, I wonder? Is he come with bell and with book to bring up the tubs? He won't make much more hand of it than he did of the ghost at 'Oods. Why, who the deuce has he got with him, and all the folks following? It's like a riot in the street. Is he going to read the Act, think ye? What's up with the people?"

"Bide still, you lazy sot!" said his mother, pushing him back into his chair. "It's difficult enough to make you get up when you 're wanted. Be quiet, I say! It's the Lieutenant and the Camelford Excise. It's nought to us. Let 'em pass by. I won't have any guffawing and staring."

The men took the hint, and remained sullenly at the table, drinking; but the procession did not pass by. It consisted of the young officer of the Curlew in his uniform,

Mr. St. Erme, several sailors belonging to the
cutter ,and half a dozen Revenue-service men,
followed by various idlers of the town ; and
it came to a full stop at the door of the Three
Crowns.

"What's your will, gentlemen?" said
Dame Brock, stepping forward, frightened at
heart, but with courtesy on her tongue. "It's
a pleasure to see his Reverence looking so
well. Can I serve you with anything?
We've the best of liquors in our cellars."

"That is exactly the point I wish to ascertain," said the Lieutenant. "I am sorry
to disturb you, Mrs. Brock ; but I have certain information that smuggled goods were
last night concealed on your premises ; and I
am legally empowered to search for such
articles of foreign produce as have not paid
duty to the Crown."

"Oh, come in, come in, Sir !" said Dame
Brock, furiously. "Don't stand outside, I
beg! Have the floors up, if you like! You're
welcome to anything that's under them. I'm
not going to fly in the face of the laws. This
is an orderly public-house. I'm known to
all the country for a woman that pays tithe
and poor-rate, as our excellent Minister can
bear witness. You have not found any fault,
or the family, I hope, with the bacon or the
home-brewed?" she added, curtseying to

the Rector. " I wish you were in better company this morning; but, anyhow, you 're an honourable gentleman. Come out, Simon! Here 's Mr. St. Erme, the Parson hisself, come down to read a bit to you."

" No, Mrs. Brock," said the clergyman, gravely, while the old man sat in the chimney corner smoking his pipe, without heeding the noise outside, or his wife's objurgations. " I am exceedingly sorry you have got yourself into this trouble. Our business is with you at the present moment, and I advise you to let it proceed quietly."

" Oh, we won't have nothing like violence here, Sir," said Dame Brock, looking round at the sullen, cowed faces of the men at the table, not one of whom had moved. " I 'm not for offering opposition to an officer wearing His Majesty's uniform, and a gentleman like yourself, one of our own county magistrates. There 's every key I possess in the world. You can search my house from garret to cellar. The furniture 's old, Sir, but I 'm not ashamed of it; and you 'll find the beds clean. If it 's not over-tidy, you 'll remember this is a busy house, and I won't say you haven't taken me completely by surprise. Walk in, I beg of ye."

" There is no need to trouble you so far," said Osborne. " If your garden gate is locked, I will thank you for that key — no other."

"Oh, you wouldn't take all these people to trample on my nice new-dug borders! You can see they've been fresh tidied up, and the seeds just shooting. What can you want there?" cried the hostess, with well-feigned astonishment. "Why, the cabbages and the taturs are coming up beautiful, and the onions springing; there's not such a crop in Lezant, unless it be in his Reverence's garden. If you'll cast your eye over, Sir, you'll see nothing can have turned the mould since the crops were put in."

"That seems true enough," said Mr. St. Erme, looking into the plot of ground opposite. "Our apples are not half so promising."

Richard Osborne, however, did not forego his purpose. He walked straight up to the gate, and, finding it unfastened, went into the garden, followed by his men.

By this time, the Three Crowns was emptied of all its occupants, except old Simon Brock. The landlady, with the ribbons of her cap streaming, and her face paler than it had been half an hour before, was already across the road.

"There's neither bolt nor bar to stop ye!" she exclaimed. "Who'd suppose gentlemen

could want to disturb a poor woman's onion-
bed and radishes? What will you do next?
There's Heaven's favour on the fruit-trees.
Such a blossoming I haven't seen these ten
years. Sure, there's nought else remarkable
in this little plot of ground. It's open to
the street, and every bit of it's took up.
We've scarce room to grow our cabbages and
carrots, as it is."

Mrs. Brock grew silent and uneasy, then
still more loquacious, when she saw the young
officer of the cutter walk steadily up to the
blooming tree at the upper extremity of the
garden, and stand still, after giving some rapid
directions to his men.

"This is more than mortal woman can
abide! If Simon wasn't paralytic, ye durstn't
do it! Dig a trench round my apple-tree!
what for, I wonder? Why, it's the glory of
the town! I don't believe the people will
let ye do it. Don't ye see that the blossom's
just setting for fruit? Touch it, one of ye, at
your peril! You'll soon know what Lezant
folk are made of, if ye do. I'm ashamed
that anybody calling himself a gentleman and
an officer should think of giving such an
order. You'll think better of it, sir!"

"Dig on, my hearties!" said Osborne,
measuring with his cane a certain space on
each side of the blooming apple-tree. "Never

fear, Dame! We won't hurt your fruit. Not
a blossom shall be injured. It will flourish
just as well at the bottom of the hill, as
on the top; and His Majesty has a fancy
to transplant it. We all work under his
orders."

There was silence among the crowd.
Even Dame Brock's eloquence failed her.
The first sound was the ring of the men's
spades striking against metal. A deep trench,
equi-distant from the tree on all sides, had by
this time been excavated; and those who
chose to look in, could see that the tree was
planted in a large square box, clamped at the
corners with iron.

"Heave it out!" Osborne said. "Let
us see what kind of crop Dame Brock rears
under her apple-tree."

The sailors were provided with ropes,
and, after another half-hour of heavy labour,
the huge box was lifted up; and a large
cavity, now filled with bales and kegs, was
brought to light. More than a hundred
casks of French brandy were ready to flavour
the dame's cider sufficiently to warm it for
winter drinking.

Osborne at once took possession of the
property in the King's name; and warning
Mrs. Brock, in spite of her violent assevera-
tions of innocence, that a heavy fine would

probably be laid upon her for harbouring contraband articles, he superintended the transfer of the goods to stores which he had engaged for the purpose.

Not the slightest opposition was made to his proceedings, as the men carried the bales down to the water's edge and returned for fresh loads; Osborne and the Rector remaining all the time in the garden. Curses, deep, but not loud, were on the lips of the smugglers, and vows of vengeance, not the less deadly that they lacked the courage and decision to break out into open resistance against the formidable party assembled to overawe them.

CHAPTER X.

MR. ST. ERME maintained his usual cold reserve, when he returned from Lezant, after
exciting the wonder of its gossips by his
public appearance, on a week-day, in the
main street. His interference caused less
anger than might have been expected among
his parishioners. His sympathies were known
not to be with them; and, though he did not
in general exert himself against the contraband traders, his principles and prejudices
were all in favour of the powers and authorities established by law.

Several days had passed since the up-
rooting of the Dame's apple-tree brought to
light one of the most cunningly-contrived of
the smugglers' hiding-places. A smothered,
but very bitter sense of injury and humilia-
tion was at work, and might be traced in the
dogged, sullen faces, of the men on the quay.
The Boscawen Arms was more unpopular
than ever: and the sailors of the cutter pa-
trolled the street, by the water-side, in front

of the storehouses that held the goods taken on the premises of the Three Crowns. At present, the wind prevailed which kept vessels from entering the harbour; and, at this season of the year, it often blew for many weeks from the same quarter.

If the Rector had been more unpopular than he really was, Mary would have been his ægis. Never had the Parsonage been more profoundly tranquil than during the soft spring evenings at the close of May, when Richard Osborne and his trusty sailors were mounting guard over the Custom-house stores; and the young officer was extending his beat after nightfall, to see that all was safe, as he walked with a quick step in the dusk past the green groves and shrubberies that overhung and encircled the clergyman's dwelling.

Mary was almost as great a stranger to her uncle as the rest of his parishioners. The shy, austere Divine had never sought to win her affection. Neither to her, nor to any human being, did that proud, reserved nature, unbend.

Yet still the young girl loved him. Every shade which crossed that high, white, wrinkled forehead, gave her pain. She saw it of late marked by fresh lines of sorrow; the pale complexion had grown still more faded; the

tall form more bent. She heard his slow
tread at a more advanced hour of the morning, as he went to the couch, which, by his
worn appearance the next day, seemed to
have afforded him no rest.

Even his step showed the disorder of
his thoughts, as he paced up and down the
garden-walk; now quickly, as if goaded by
the reflections that preyed upon his mind;
now tardily, as if heavy with the weight of
years and care. Yet Reginald St. Erme, who
had for so long been irreverently styled by
his uncourteous flock, " our old Parson," was
not really an aged man.

That tall, wiry frame, still had strength
dwelling in its muscles; the trembling of
the hands, which gave such a semblance of
feebleness, arose more from feverish impatience than from infirmity of constitution.
There might be—he sometimes feared there
were—long years of the life of which he
was weary, in store for him. The principles
which still warred against temptation, but
were hardly strong enough to maintain the
strife, wavered in yet darker moments, and
scarcely restrained this man of ascetic habits,
and outwardly unblemished life, from abruptly cutting short the thread of an existence, which seemed to him, in his bitterness

of spirit, valueless to others and burdensome to himself.

To one who, like Mary, watched him anxiously, there was a change, fraught with terrible significancy, in the spirit of the discourses which fell on the unlistening or wondering ears of his congregation, like the thin mist which hardly leaves behind it, when the sun breaks forth, a trace of its having passed over the earth. She listened with dread to the frequent occurrence of phrases referring, dimly indeed, to the spiritual agency of mysterious supernatural powers, quite distinct from the workings of Divine Providence. Some of the elderly men, after trying to comprehend these dreamy, rhapsodical harangues, went home and said, Sure, the old Passon was crazed; they could make no meaning at all, now, out of his long-winded sermons. Others, again, declared that, even in the pulpit, he was fighting with the Enemy; not as he is wont to be dealt with by divines of sound mind, but holding dialogues and controversies with the Evil Spirit, in which, it was the opinion of the villagers, that the Parson was like to come off the worst. He was sore troubled, the old women said, and made so many words about the matter he had in hand, that they knew less about it when he left off than when he began. It was not Scripture truth he taught, but just his own odd fancies; more like what might be found in a conjuring-book, than the parables and allegories he used to expound to them.

In their own home, his niece thought there was another change, of a quite different nature, in his manner. He would fix his eyes upon her without speaking, but so wistfully that she longed to throw her arms round his neck, and ask him what she could do to ease him of his troubles. His habitual reserve made it impossible for her to venture upon such demonstrations of affection. Never in her whole life had she dared to break through the bonds of their formal but not unkindly intercourse. These pressed upon her most in his presence. When he was shut up in his own room she would form hardy resolutions, and determine to put them into execution; but the moment she saw him again, the influence of early habit re-asserted its claim.

Often she stood at the door of his study, with her hand upon the latch, not daring to raise it, listening to his restless tread, as he walked up and down, sometimes talking aloud, though she knew him to be quite alone. Then came pauses, as if to allow the invisible guest he had been addressing time to answer him. Dead silence prevailed, unless he was speaking;

yet when he raised his voice again, it seemed to the anxious girl as though he were making replies, or asking brief questions.

Mr. St. Erme and his niece were sitting alone together, as was their wont, for some hours of the evening, before he shut himself in his study. Mary's heart beat when, as she occasionally looked up from her work, she met his gaze fixed upon her, with that earnest wistful expression she had often seen in it of late. He did not speak to her, but neither did he avert his eyes when she raised her head. She scarcely knew whether, in reality, his thoughts might not be far away.

Hers was a face on which it was pleasant to dwell; but in general its fair tint and regularity of feature attracted little of his attention. He had not thought until now, when circumstances gave weight to the consideration, how much purity and goodness was expressed in the young girl's calm, somewhat mournful countenance.

They had been silent for so long —habitually, he was so chary of his words—that Mary started when her uncle said,—

" The world has seemed to me peopled with phantoms, lately! This old house appears to be less our own than the property of the dead. Is it only to me that the rooms, the garden-walks, even the church, seem haunted? Forms enter and take their once accustomed places, without exciting wonder or comment, although for years they have not visited us. Is it because I live so much alone, in prayer and meditation, among my books, that these manifestations of the spiritual world are accorded to me? Are they never present with you?"

He bent his head as he spoke and looked at her fixedly, while a frown furrowed his brow.

" You are not well, dear uncle Reginald," said Mary, with affectionate respect. "Indeed, I would be very still if you allowed me to be oftener with you. Hour after hour, you are shut up in your study, with sad thoughts, I fear, for your companions. I, too, am dreary enough, at times," she observed, while her soft eyes filled with tears. "Strange fancies —yearnings for the lost, fill my heart; but I can hardly remember those dearest to me. I think, if I could recall them more plainly, me- mory would bring their images before me so vividly that, like yourself, I should not know whether they were real."

" Keep to that thought! Let it be with you constantly. You will see them sooner or later. The dead are all around us, Mary," said Mr. St. Erme, still bending forward, while his voice, though low, thrilled through the nerves of the listener. "I see them—I hear their footsteps. You do not sit up late enough, or wake as I do, when the drowsy world is yet asleep. These appearances must be courted. They are coy, and, if neglected, soon vanish. Yes," he added, bitterly, "before we have learned what they come from the world of spirits to tell us."

Mary listened to him, terrified by his strange words, and the subdued excitement of his manner.

"You are young," he said; "fresh and pure as the dewy grass on which I sometimes trace the footprints of the invisible ones. Oh! if I could see with your eyes, hear with your ears, clearer manifestations might be granted to me! Sorrow has deadened my perceptions; sins, many and grievous, clog my faculties. Of late they have been very dull—almost dead within me. Few, comparatively, distinct communications from the unseen world, which lies but at a short distance from us—if, indeed, we are separated thence by more than the gross material of the body, in which our finer senses are shrouded —hardly any record, I repeat, can be found of a message from a departed spirit being transmitted, except through the medium of a youth or a maiden. It must be a fine organ that can hear the voices breathing constantly around us, unheard by dull mortal ears; voices which are saying, could they but make the sound intelligible to us, what we would give more than life to know."

Terror at his apparent madness, pity, holy and tender as an angel's, overcame Mary's accustomed timidity. She drew nearer to her uncle, and tried to take his hand, but he did not respond to the mute caress.

" Let me suppose you acquainted," he said, after a momentary pause, " with the terrible features of your unhappy father's destiny. Speak, if what I utter is unintelligible; but spare me as much as may be. A month ago I went to the old Manor-house, deep sunk among Lord Boscawen's woods. I believed it to be my especial duty to set at rest the evil reports that hung about the place, and put an end to sights and sounds which filled its inmates with horror. Mary, what I saw and heard on that fearful night made my hair whiter than eighteen years of sorrow had done. I had always believed that Fleming, in a fit of drunken delirium, had with his own hand terminated his wretched existence. I do not hold that conviction now. I went in the strength of that confidence which the fiercest trials had not shaken. I had armed myself with spiritual weapons. With the prayers of the Church—the armour to which I was accustomed—about me, I betook myself to conflict with the Evil One. In that battle I was overthrown."

Mary's eyes dilated with terror. She looked, with anguish in her young face, at the convulsed features of her uncle, but she did not interrupt him.

"By my own wish," Mr. St. Erme continued, "I was shut up, the door locked, and I was left to pass the night in the ghost chamber, as it is called—the haunted room at Woods. I heard the wind whistling in the corridors, the swaying of the close-set trees round the old building, the creaking of the branches, and the hooting of the owls; and, for some time, nothing more. My nerves were stiller than is often the case now. The usual manifestation of a spiritual presence did not appear to me to be in the air. Suddenly, when my mind was calmest and clearest, I heard the sound of voices, now angry, now mocking and bitterly derisive; not in the gallery, nor under the windows, but seemingly close beside me. I rose and searched the chamber, but, though I still heard those waves of sound rising and falling, I could see no one, nor was I able to distinguish a single word. I called upon the unearthly beings who were, I began to think, around me, but none responded. The same hellish gabble filled the room, and my solemn adjurations were disregarded; laughter and derision silenced them.

"A great anguish fell upon me. I looked upward, and my eyes were arrested by a picture which hung high over the mantel-piece. The divine tranquillity of the Madonna's countenance seemed to reassure me. Had I been a Roman Catholic, I should have prayed to her for aid. The features somewhat reminded me of your own."

He looked down, with more affection than he was wont to display, on the young girl.

Mary did not speak, or for a moment withdraw her gaze from his face. Her soul seemed to have passed into his—her very life to hang upon his words.

"While my eyes were fixed upon the painting, the canvas moved, and slowly the image of the Virgin seemed drawn away, revealing a gloomy aperture. As I looked closely, there gradually loomed upon me from the darkness a form and features which I never can forget. They belonged, Mary, to the man who was found lying, eighteen years ago, murdered, or a suicide, at the foot of Lezant Cliff. So menacing, so terrible was his expression, that, for the first time that night, my courage failed me; I could have hidden myself in the earth to escape poor

Fleming's glance. Pale as I had seen him lying dead, when I was summoned to view the corpse—when my quiet life was broken in upon by a woe which has not yet worn itself out—I saw him confront me. 'Speak!' I said to the ghastly phantom. 'Tell me, in the name of the Eternal Being, before whom one day we must both stand, who did that cruel deed?' but no answer came. The vision lasted but for a moment, yet, while there, it seemed to scorch my eyeballs; I covered them with my hands, involuntarily: when I looked again, the picture of the Madonna was in its place."

There was a dark rim round the girl's eyes — unutterable agony in her glance. The delusion, if it were one, under which he laboured, seemed fast possessing her. "Would that I had been there!" she said. "Me, those foul fiends should not have deceived. Why did you not call on *him*, my father? Surely, the spirits were all about you."

Mr. St. Erme looked round him nervously in the darkening twilight. "I did so," he answered, in a whisper; "I called upon Edmund, and I thought, I fancied there was a stir in the chamber; the air seemed cleft, but my ears could not distinguish the sound. Mary," he said, in a tone of anguish, "as truly as you are now near me in the flesh, I believe that Edmund's tortured soul was striving to make an intelligible utterance, and that I was unfit to receive it. I have been an unworthy minister of the Gospel. There have been souls in this parish, aye, even in my own family, lost through my negligence. I tread upon the verge of the spiritual world. Heroes, philosophers, poets, the mighty spectres of past ages, visit me; but those whom I most covet to approach hold themselves aloof; my own dead will not come when I summon them! And yet, Mary, only a few nights since, as I was walking in the garden, I heard, as plainly as I now hear the breath part from your quivering lips, a deep, impassioned, gasping sigh. Edmund was near me then;—I felt his presence, though I did not with my bodily eyes see him;—I knew that he was only divided by a few brief paces from me."

His tone was now so calm and quiet, that Mary, for an instant, imagined that the belief he expressed arose from some more real cause than the strange flights of half-mad enthusiasm to which she had been listening.

"Are you certain," she said, "that my father is dead? I never heard it before."

Mr. St. Erme gazed at her compassionately. "Believe it now," he answered. "Many years ago, information was conveyed to me from the highest quarter, that, in attempting to make his escape from his place of confinement, my unfortunate brother perished. If I had not known it earlier, that hour would have told it to me. Nothing but his being near me in the spirit could have so stirred my inmost soul. Mary, it is thus that friends we have lost manifest themselves to us after death, imperfectly. We hear a footfall —a sigh reaches us; but we hear no words; they seem to touch us with their trailing garments; our senses, inadequate as they are, are filled with that mysterious presence; and then we are left in our restlessness alone, unsatisfied, yearning for a fuller insight into what has been so darkly revealed."

His countenance clouded over, and he sighed deeply. Mary's usually calm, melancholy face, showed an extraordinary emotion. Her eyes seemed irradiated; the colour rose warmly in her cheek, as she said,—

"It needs no message from the unseen world to tell me what is stamped upon my heart. Richard has the same perfect confidence. Uncle, there is one fault upon my conscience; let me confess it to you. I have seen my brother, contrary to your orders. He is bent upon publicly establishing the fact that my father was not guilty. Might he not aid us?"

Mr. St. Erme remained silent for some moments.

"Do not ask me to receive him, Mary. Richard has disobeyed me. I believe his coming to this place to be an ill-advised measure. Much consideration has been shown to us; and had I been consulted, this appointment, for which, I have little doubt, he eagerly sought, would have been given to another. Yet the workings of Providence are mysterious. It may be as the means to an end which, at present, I do not perceive, that you have been brought together. But remember, no human affection can sustain us in these trials. Read the lives of women who have been set apart—purged, as it were, by fire and water—pierced through with the sharp arrows of affliction, before they were fitted to perform their allotted tasks. Let such be your models. Pride, vanity, soft living, all must be given up. The recipient of such communications as I would have you hold yourself in readiness to entertain, must be pure in heart, and most strict in life. You are young; as yet you have not been led into temptation. It is possible that your father's innocence of the dreadful crime he was accused of having committed may be proved by you."

Mary promised to obey him. Long after nightfall, they paced together, more lovingly than had ever been the case, the pathways of the Rector's garden, while the deep shadows unrolled themselves over land and sea; and the girl sometimes started as the bats flew past her face, and fancied that she heard, close behind her, the sound of footsteps. Mr. St. Erme, the floodgates of his mind once opened, poured forth strange experiences, wild theories, wistful regrets, until the garden-walks seemed peopled with forms of those lost and gone before, which were more real to him than the substantial shapes of everyday life.

For many hours after she left her uncle, Mary's thoughts were almost as wild and wandering as his own. Her whole life was a preparation for a holier state, and that night the fervency of her prayers was doubled. Gradually, her emotions became subdued; and when the morning broke, and the early sunbeams sparkled on the window of her room, looking to the east, where she had slept since she was a child, she was slumbering peacefully, with tears glistening on her long eyelashes, and as innocent an expression on her young face as it had worn when, almost an infant, she first wept herself to rest after hearing, without understanding the misery which had fallen upon her, that she was to see no more of her kind, handsome, indulgent father.

CHAPTER XI.

THE young French girl had been very restless ever since Jacob Mohr offered her a passage back to France in the schooner. England had by no means answered her expectations. There were moments when she thought that she had left all her life's happiness behind her on the banks of the Rance. The shadowy woodland, through which, at first, bright vistas of enjoyment seemed to open, now closed in oppressively around her. She no longer mistook the distant stems of the birch-trees, as the wind swayed them to and fro, for moving figures; nor the shrill cries of the jay and the plover for a seaman's whistle.

Even the farm life, in which Reine felt disposed to take an active part, did not greatly enliven her. Mrs. Helier left everything to Leah; and, except in upsetting the pails of milk, and disturbing the pans of cream, of which they were as fond as the cats that followed them about, the girls showed no disposition to take any share in what was going forward. They would torment the cows till the patient animals turned upon the impish creatures and drove them from the yard; or they set the dogs to chase the pigs, and screamed with laughter when the little savage terrier puppies worried the poor beasts cruelly; but there was no gladness in their mirth. Reine felt a cold shiver run through her veins, when she saw them heartlessly sporting with the sufferings of dumb animals, enjoying the cruel play of the cats with the young birds and mice, and stringing the eggs out of the rifled nests of the thrushes and linnets.

In that house there was so much that was ill or inadequately performed, that the old servant, Leah, gradually grew to feel a sort of respect for the young foreigner, who got through more work in a day than the mistress, with all her groaning and rocking, would finish in a month. Reine's marvellously neat French caps and aprons, the small frillings and elaborate stitchings of her underclothing, the dexterity of her darning and fitting, excited the woman's admiration, the more especially because it was a department in which she made no pretence of excelling. Awful were the holes in the frocks and petticoats, and terrible the gaps in the cotton stockings of the awkward girls, who lived a wild life among bushes and briers, and never thought of rectifying the injuries inflicted on their garments by the sharp brambles.

Now and then, disgusted by her mistress's tardiness, the woman, who had nursed these children in infancy, without loving them, would put some awkward stitches in their clothes, which made the rents look more unsightly than before—like a hole in a quickset hedge, stopped up with a barren network of thorns. Bad as her work was, it caused the articles thus mended to hang together during the somewhat rough ordeal of the great monthly wash; but it was a wonder to see the Breton lass restoring some delicate bit of lace or muslin with stitches that could scarcely be distinguished from the original fabric, and getting over the ground as swiftly with her fine cotton, as the gigantic strides and leaps of the housekeeper's large needle could carry her coarse thread. Reine's quick perception soon taught her also to modulate her French accent and idiom. She had picked up more English, Leah said, in a fortnight, than her master seemed likely to gain in a lifetime.

There had been a period when Mrs. Helier's state of health and spirits was worse than at present, and the children were, in consequence, removed from her, and placed abroad. Now she seemed, generally, like

the other inmates of Woods, according to
Leah, only half awake. Many a fine day
passed without her mistress's moving from her
chair. The girls, if they were not in mischief, lay about in the sunny weather under
hayricks, sleeping away their time. No one
was busy but herself. The master did his
work with his eyes shut, and was cheated
right and left. He might have been a gentleman, by the way he left his business to
others; mooning about the fields with his
hands behind his back, and blinking like the
owls at the March dust, when other farmers
thought it worth a king's ransom. The land
was exhausted, and yielded nothing like a
decent crop. The cows were half-starved,
and allowed to feed on what they could pick
up. Their butter fetched less at Lezant than
that churned in other dairies; and the quan-
tity, what with waste and mismanagement,
was not half what it ought to be.

Reine thought of the old housekeeper's
grumbling remarks whenever the family were
assembled. The most simple task was too
difficult for the unskilled fingers of the girls;
and their mother would sit with a basket full
of untouched, homely, household needlework
before her, rocking herself in her chair, with
a dreary sound, as the bare oak flooring
responded to the movement. Mr. Helier de-

tested noise of all kinds, and would frown and storm till his wife left off this, her solitary recreation. Sometimes, in spite of her abject fears of his temper, she would begin again, unconsciously, swaying herself backward and forward in some dim, far-off corner of the large old room, till a violent objurgation reduced her to absolute stillness.

Reine was perfectly at liberty to indulge in her own sad thoughts during the rambles she took with the children, who were nominally her charge, after the slight tasks she tried to set them were over; for the wind, perpetually sweeping over the moor, would have been almost as easy to trace as to follow the erratic course of these half-mad creatures. They came back to her, however, occasionally, panting and out of breath, with their thin, fair hair dishevelled by the blast; much in the same manner that dogs, after ranging the upland, come to their master's side to receive, as it may happen, caress or chiding.

They were not bad guides, after all, for every path was familiar to them; and even when out of sight, Reine heard their elfish shrieks and laughter, as they alternately played together and quarrelled, chased each other over the downs, or hid themselves in fun behind the tree-trunks in the woodland, starting out and screaming wildly when discovered.

Reine saw them far down below, on the seashore, one day, when she came over the green hill to the south-west of Woods, and followed the course of a treeless defile, leading to the coast. All her efforts to penetrate, in that direction, the thicket which lined the ravine, had been vain; but when the girls found how much she longed for a nearer view of the blue water, they had shown her this way down to the sands. Her heart beat as she heard the long surging roll of the waves dashing against the headlands, and saw the cliffs extending, like frowning buttresses, far as the eye could reach.

A streamlet flowed down the glen, between beds of moss and cresses, vividly green and sparkling with moisture. Slabs of granite chequered the turf; but the face of the cliffs exposed to the Atlantic waves was black as night, splintered and jagged by the perpetual action of the ground-swell and heavy sea, as well as hollowed into caverns, which, however, owing to the depth of water close inland, afforded no refuge or chance of escape to the shipwrecked wretch thrown by those gloomy billows, in their angry play, upon that awful coast. Even now, in sunshine, and with a soft spring wind blowing from the south, the mighty rollers looked dark and threatening, until they broke in white foam upon the rocks, with a sound that swelled into thunder as it was reverberated from the arched recesses of the cliffs.

Standing out to sea, but connected with a farther peninsula or island by an isthmus, against which the stormy tides were constantly making assault, was a great bluff, whereon might be traced the remains of a strong fortress. Nothing ornamental clung to the dark stonework, which, as it jutted irregularly above the turf, might have been taken for slabs of slate. Not a sprig of ivy, no lichens or mosses, hung on the walls of the unprotected ruin, over which the cruel north-west wind from the Atlantic had swept for centuries; but popular tradition had preserved many a tale and legend of the old Castle, in which it was said the great British monarch, with his band of trusty knights, had feasted gaily, and whence he had gone forth, with his good sword Escalibar at his side, to the dreadful battle-field, from which he was to return no more.

Reine was too much of a stranger in the country to be well acquainted with its antiquities; but the name of King Arthur's Castle suggested part, at least, of its story to the Breton girl. She mounted, not without difficulty, the zigzag flight of broken steps connecting the island, on which some portion of the fortress was still to be traced, with the bluff whereon parts of the portal arch, the keep and outer wall, in their rude strength, had defied the attacks of time.

Over the lonely ruin, black and bare, the sea-birds were swooping, hardly to be scared by the footfall of a human being, from a place which must have seemed their own, so seldom was it visited. As they took flight, the white wings of the gulls brushed close past her; their hoarse screaming sounded in her ear; while, on all sides, the dash of the waves against the dark masses of the rock bewildered Reine's senses. She looked down to see how far off the young girls had wandered, and beheld them, like specks upon the beach, clambering among the stones with which it was strewn. Reine walked to the other side of the island, and was gazing out upon the turbulent waters which had worked such marvels, and wrought into such stupendous shapes those black towers and battlements of slate, when the shadow of a man's figure, thrown across the stone on which she was resting, showed that Richard Osborne was leaning over her.

Reine did not turn or speak, though her colour varied, and a bright gleam sparkled in the eyes so sedulously averted.

"Ma mie, ma douce mie!" said Osborne, addressing her by the fond caressing term once frequently used between them, and trying to take her hand. "Have you forgotten me?"

Reine turned her sparkling glance full upon him.

"Yes!" she said. "England is different from France. Those who were friends on the banks of the Rance, do not know each other on these cold black cliffs. I am but following the fashion of your country. I do not like its manners, however," she continued, hurriedly, as if to prevent his answering her. "Very soon—in another month, perhaps—I shall be gone. The Captain who brought me here, will take me back to Brittany."

Osborne's countenance became grave as he listened to her.

"You are going with that smuggling rascal in La Belle Marie? with his crew— Dutch, French, English, I know not what,— but all vagabonds! ·Reine, that must not be."

"How dare you contradict me?" said the French girl, with vivacity. "What right have you to prescribe to me the company I shall keep, the friends I like to favour? Once I thought as you do about the smuggling; but I have changed my mind now. All people alter when their foot touches English soil. Why not I?"

"I am not changed, Reine!" said the

young man, in a tone of deep feeling; while, at the same time, a degree of embarrassment, caused by circumstances which he could not confide to her, restrained the avowal of strong affection hovering on his lips. "I wish I could remove you at once from the place and people among whom you have thrown yourself; but my prospects are darker than ever. At this moment I have not a home to offer you. My very name — always obscure — is scarcely my own. Will you not wait, be constant, trust me, till I have carved out a destiny which you may share?"

"I would not trust you for one hour, one minute!" said the girl, passionately. "Before the sun dipped into the sea—ere you were half way to Lezant—you would have betrayed, forgotten me — perhaps made my name your sport. Go, Monsieur! I release you; I give you back your troth-plight. Do as you like! The Breton girl will not keep you an unwilling prisoner."

She rose, and tried to pass him; but Osborne caught her hands, and held them fast.

"Reine!" he said, "be patient with me. It has not been in my power to seek you out at Woods, and you failed in keeping the tryst I had appointed. This is not the first time I have visited Arthur's Castle."

" Ah, that was not my fault!" said Reine,
eagerly. " Your note was en retard—too
late. I did not get it till the evening when
your cutter sailed out of Lezant Harbour."

" So far, so good!" said the Lieutenant,
cheerfully. " No matter, since we have met
here at last. Chance has been kinder to me
than you are. Tell me, Reine! did no
thought, no recollection, that we were to have
been at this spot together, bring you here
to-day?"

" No, no! I thought you were gone.
News does not fly fast in those woods," said
Reine. " I would not have come here if I
had known you were in the country. Ces
enfans, where are they? It was to oblige
them I came. Why, the cutter sailed on
Saturday!"

" Yes!" said Osborne, frowning darkly.
" I was beguiled into the belief that the
smuggling schooner's cargo was to be landed
up the Channel; while, in reality, my departure left this coast clear for their venture.
Reine, these are desperate scoundrels! Sooner
or later, punishment will overtake them. I
must be vigilant and stern, and I believe they
will not escape me. When did the skipper
make you the offer you mentioned a few
minutes since? Is he off the coast still?"

Reine looked at him fixedly. " If you

think to learn the secrets of Jacob Mohr or
Lance Fleming from me," she said, firmly,
"you are mistaken. They are my friends.
I will not betray them."

"How can you call these lawless men
your friends, Reine?" said the young Lieutenant. "Even your childhood in 'la belle
France' may have taught you what smuggling
is,—the vices to which it leads. I have
heard you speak of them with horror."

"No matter!" replied the young girl,
abruptly. "Jacob Mohr has been kind to
me. I was happy on board his vessel—more
so than I am likely to be again. I love every
plank of La Belle Marie — the little ship
which brought me to England. Ah, I was
without care then! The waves rocked me to
sleep not less sound because her cargo had
not paid duty. I am glad he landed it
safely."

"Half was captured last week. The rest
will be ours shortly," said Osborne, in an
offended tone. "You may repeat my words
to your friends, if you like, Reine; and depend
upon it, if they fall into my hands they shall
meet with small mercy. But be warned!
You cannot break off this connexion too soon.
Neither Jacob Mohr nor Lance Fleming is to
be trusted. They have no law but their own
wild will. The house where you live is not

safe. I do not believe a word of the idle stories about its being haunted by spirits. One as guileless as yourself told me that the consciences of bad men, troubled by crimes, often woke such semblances; but neither is that altogether my meaning. Woods has been for years a hiding-place for smuggled goods. One lot I unearthed a few nights ago; this soil will disgorge more before I have done. Your host is weak in mind and body; he cannot protect you; and the very walls of your chamber may be lined and perforated with secret passages and cavities. You must not stay there."

"That is not your business!" said Reine, her colour rising angrily. "Les revenants— what is it you call them? — do not frighten me; nor am I apprehensive that the old passages and crumbling walls of the house where I reside harbour living foes. My conscience is tranquil, for I have no enemies, and do not mean to defy those with whom I dwell. Adieu! That fair being, of whom you spoke but now, will console you for losing me."

She darted away as she spoke, descending quickly the rocky steps which she had mounted with difficulty. Osborne followed her, but she would not accept his offers of assistance.

The girls, who had been plucking the starry trefoil which grew in the interstices of the cliffs, and trying vainly to climb high enough to reach the samphire clinging to the rocks overhead, were sitting waiting for her, picking up pebbles, and casting them out to sea, in emulation which could throw farthest.

They stared at Osborne, but did not speak. He saluted them coldly, hardly noticing their strange appearance. Reine's jealousy, which he was beginning to guess at, pleased while it troubled him. He could not, at the present moment, set her fears at rest; but he rejoiced at discovering that the change in her manner arose, not from faithlessness or insensibility, but from believing herself slighted for the sake of another.

"Farewell, then, Mademoiselle!" he said, at last, after, with somewhat distracted thoughts, he had striven in vain to conciliate her. "You will own, some day, that you have misjudged me. I must wait till that happy time arrives. I have only one more request to urge,—Do not return to France in La Belle Marie!"

The girls looked up at him with their sharp eyes, as he distinctly and slowly uttered the last words. Reine would have given the world to keep him near her, but pride restrained her. He lingered, held out his hand, but she did not look up, and he left her.

Reine's glance followed him involuntarily, as he went by the course of the stream up the valley at a quick firm pace, without once looking back. She knew that he would stop when he reached the bend in the hills which must hide him from her view; but she did not turn away her head, and he was satisfied when he saw by her attitude that she was watching him. He waved his hand; then springing up the abrupt side of the down, he pursued his way. Reine's thoughts accompanied his every footstep; and, now that he was gone, the recollection of his clear, truthful eye and voice, seemed to convince her better of his constancy than his words had done while he was near her. When he was out of sight, she got up, and followed by the girls, who were weary and footsore after their scramble among the sharp-pointed flints, she went thoughtfully but with fewer jealous misgivings up the steep defile. The children stole into the house furtively, to avoid a scolding from Leah for their boots, spoiled by the stones and sea-water, and torn and draggled petticoats. Reine sat listening in appearance to the housekeeper's chronicles of the old British fortress that lay in ruins near them, while in reality she was recalling every syllable addressed to her by her lover. Leah attributed her silence to weariness.

Richard Osborne, with his foreign associations derived from his youth spent abroad,
felt more than ever like a stranger in his
native land as he walked back to Lezant.
Disappointed in the result of the interview
which at first promised so much—conscious
that his mysterious conduct might have given
Reine cause for jealousy, and shaken her belief
in his affection, the young officer slackened
his pace gradually, pausing and pondering as
he crossed the headlands and descended into the
dusky combes, over and through which led
the pathway that Morgan Price had warned
him was especially dangerous ground for him
to tread.

Lance Fleming did not see Reine at first,
when he went home that night, while she was
still sitting in a shadowy nook of the housekeeper's warm, cheerful parlour. He lifted
the latch of the outer door suddenly, and
stayed for a few minutes talking to Leah, who
was anxious to know how Dame Brock and
the Lezant folk bore the loss of their share of
La Belle Marie's last cargo.

"Some say the bales are as much their
own as ever," said Lance; "but they are
boasting fellows at the Three Crowns, and
will never show pluck enough for a fair fight
with the Excise. Andrew swears the stores
shall be set on fire, and the new brick and

mortar pulled to pieces, before a single article
is carried on board the cutter. At all events,
she cannot come round to take them off while
this south-east wind blows. Her officer is
very foolhardy. Would you believe it, Leah,
as I came from Lezant, where his name was
in every man's mouth, I saw the Lieutenant
coming alone over the headland—just crossing that beetling cliff where my father met his
death!"

He drew his breath hard, and stopped abruptly. Leah looked at him anxiously. " I
hope he came to no harm," she said. " What
put that thought in your head, Master Lance?
It is an ill-omened place."

" He had a narrow escape," said Lance.
"I did not feel in charity with him myself,
and there were others not far off whose blood
was on fire after the loss of the kegs. They
would have made little scruple about jostling
against him in the dusk, and shoving him over
the cliff. I had no reason to be his friend.
For that matter, there were tales told in
Lezant market to-day that maddened me.
When he and the old Parson stood together
under Dame Brock's apple-tree — I don't
know what else brought our parish-priest out
of his cell—all Lezant was staring at them,
and finding out a likeness in their features.
Well, when I saw him coming over that blood-

stained cliff, with that light, arrogant step of
his, as if the earth was not good enough to
tread upon, I believed those stories to be true.
Just so, perhaps, with that careless, dare-devil
air, the gay Colonel came upon my father.
True or false, there was a look in his face as
he fronted me on the headland which belongs
only to one family hereabouts. I mean, the
St. Ermes."

His voice lost its menacing tone as he
caught sight of Reine's pale, anguish-stricken
countenance. Lance stood in the doorway,
looking proud and animated, with a flush
upon his cheek and a light glittering in his
eye as he proceeded,—

"I will not say that I might not have
spoken my warning more civilly, when I told
the Lieutenant, if he valued his safety, to
make haste to his night's quarters ; but he
gave me back the discourtesy, whatever it was,
and we parted worse friends than before. He
walked on carelessly, stopping every now and
then to look out to sea, or towards the ravine
at Woods, and heeding neither the enemy he
had just made for himself behind his back,
nor half-a-dozen of the worst fellows in the
town, who were coming to meet us up the
pathway from the old inn. They were jeering
and threatening him, as soon as they saw what
man it was that stood in their way, and must

pass, unless he bolted off the course, between them and the most dangerous gap in the cliff. I did not like their looks, and, though I had been angry before, I went on quicker, to make the game even. Six to one was unfair odds, even though no doubt the officer carried pistols.

" He had his hand inside the breast of his coat, as if aware of his danger, and, leaving off his musings, walked steadily on. Just as the men went up the path with a run as if in sport, but spreading themselves out so as to take up the whole of the narrow space, the small gate opening out upon the cliff from Mr. St. Erme's grounds was unlocked, and while the wind sent a gush of scent from the Parson's May-trees on the air, a white form came forth, and took her way through the midst of us, to meet the Lieutenant. We all of us knew her. It was Colonel St. Erme's daughter."

Lance paused;—he seemed to be lost in thought. " I believe that I never really looked at her before," he said, slowly. " Why, Leah! the angels in heaven are not more beautiful. She came among those half-drunk, mischievously-inclined sinners, as unfearingly as if she bore a charmed life, and nothing could harm her. I scarcely think she saw them, though she did the best thing, had she guessed their intentions, to save her brother.

"Yes," he went on, presently, "they are both Colonel St. Erme's children! I knew it, as they stood together on the cliff. The same light, lofty gait, the same haughty eye, though her glance is softened by religion and sorrow. The men were in a noisy humour, but they all shrank back abashed when the young lady placed her small white fingers on the Lieutenant's arm, and led him through the midst of the angry brawlers. It was like a spirit of light rebuking deeds of darkness. Richard Osborne was safe from that instant. But he should take care. She may not always stand between him and the edge of the precipice."

Lance took down a candle from a shelf, and, without bidding Reine or Leah goodnight, went to his own room. Both the women noticed that a change had taken place in his manner. There was more intelligence in his handsome features, more dignity in the carriage of the small, well-poised head. His lounging, careless gait was steadied. The impression produced by the past scene had evidently roused the latent spirit of the man of gentle blood within him.

"What ails the lad?" said Leah, wonderingly. "He looks like one that has had a philtre from the fairies! That blast he spoke of has bewitched him. There's nothing so unwholesome as the smell of the hawthorn; if you bring it into a dwelling, it breeds fevers. How his eyes glimmered! and he carried his head higher than his poor father bore himself, before he began to take that which sunk him. Lance is wild, too, but I don't think he'll follow in his footsteps."

Leah sighed as she went about her work; and Reine, glad to be alone, withdrew to her own chamber. Very little ceremony was required to be observed in the family. Sometimes, for days, she did not see Mr. or Mrs. Helier. The master had been more brisk than usual that afternoon, Leah said, but had tired himself riding about, and was gone to bed early. Mrs. Helier was poorly, and had not quitted her room. As for the children, they were not fit to be seen, and she had put them to bed as soon as she had caught sight of them.

Reine, though she lay down, could not sleep; or, if slumber for a moment weighed down her eyelids, she started up, imagining Richard in the power of the smugglers, who were hurling him from the edge of the beetling headland. The young, warm-hearted girl loved him the better for his misfortunes, if Lance's assertion that he was the son of

Colonel St. Erme should prove to be correct.
She longed to speak comfort to him. Her own
harsh, ungentle behaviour was remembered
with compunction, contrasted with the quiet,
yet lofty bearing of the fair, delicate girl — so
like him, nevertheless, as to proclaim their
kindred — who had constrained even that
rude, lawless band to respect her presence,
and awed their vindictive passions into sub-
mission.

CHAPTER XII.

LEAH SCRIVEN's bees hummed cheerily under the wall, where the hives stood in goodly order; and, in the breaches of the broken stonework at the corner, a flourishing crop of snapdragon and wild rockets had sprung up. Reine, with a heart lighter than it had been for the last fortnight, was singing, as she plied her needle in the pleasant shade cast by the old trees. Her sanguine fancies had once more revived; her ears were open to every passing sound. Now that her jealous misgivings were put to rest, it seemed as if some mysterious agency must be at work to bring together those a cruel fate had severed, and between whom the seeds of dissension had been sown.

She was still sitting on the mossy bench under the old apple-trees, when a small arched door in the ivied wall opened, and Leah came into the orchard. A vivid gleam of sunlight stole through the portal, revealing glimpses of a paved court beyond, strewn with stones and mortar,

which had fallen from the most ancient portion
of the building. The high roofs and chimneys
of the Manor-house rose on the farther side,
above the mounds of rubbish, and one large
mullioned window, set in a lofty peaked gable,
looked down upon the dreary enclosure.

"Did you see anything, ma'amselle?"
Leah said, sharply, as she came back from
gathering herbs in the warm corner near the
beehives. "This is a dismal spot; but it is
too early in the day to be fearful. What
makes you look at that old window so
long?"

"Only because it is such a quaint, fanci-
ful bit of sculpture. We have many houses
in our French towns, which hang out their
upper windows over the narrow streets in that
fashion. It is not so *triste* to me here for
that reason. No, I see nothing to frighten
me; nothing but the swallows flying about,
and the tendrils of ivy waving in the breeze.
Is that only the wind I hear?—how strangely
sweet it sounds!"

The women both listened, and Leah
turned somewhat pale, as a gush of low-
toned, indistinct melody seemed to issue from
the grey, shadowy wing of the ancient house.
It might be, as Reine had said, only the wind
sighing in the deep embrasures, and rustling
among the ivy leaves flapping against the

wall, but the sound appeared more sustained and thrilling.

"That is what my mother used to call the French lady's song," Leah said, coming closer to Reine, and speaking in a subdued whisper. "Sometimes I think of what she used to tell me about her, when I hear you singing your scraps of music, which have no meaning to me, about the place. Mother lived here while she was a girl, in old Lord Boscawen's time—he who built the great range of stables yonder, that look as ruinous now as the rest. Nothing prospers about some houses; and part of the material used was very ancient, and part unseasoned; it was all done in a hurry, to please my lord, who wanted to have his hunters down, and couldn't wait. He was a daring, wicked man, and thought of nothing but his own pleasures, his hunting and shooting; the best horseman he was, I have heard, in his day, in all the country side. He never kept much company here; there was a reason for that—the poor young French lady that lived with him, and saw nobody. Perhaps I ought not to tell you about her; but it was more than forty years ago, and my lord is a white-haired old man, past fourscore; so it will do no harm if I say my say. Every one was sorry for her; she used to drive her white ponies up and down the green lanes, and in lonely places, and still, folks say, you may hear the sound of the wheels. When the wind plays through the bars of that old window, it seems as if she might be sitting behind the blind, as my mother would describe her, playing the harpsichord, with her fingers, and even her small thumb, covered with rings.''

Reine's countenance showed an unusual degree of interest. "Eh bien ! this poor foreign lady—what became of her ? Was she here when the great fire was raging, which, you told me the other day, burned down the chapel and offices ?"

" Yes, she was here then ; but, strange to say, she was never seen afterwards. Some thought my lord was tired of the connexion, and fired the place to get rid of her; others, that he bribed the captain of a privateering vessel to carry her away with him : men in cloaks, jabbering French, were said to have come about the place. Those were distracted times. There was talk of an invasion. The King's crown was scarce set fast on his head ; and as for the revenue, 'twas but little he got of it. The smuggling you've seen was nothing to what went on then.

" My mother always believed that Madame was taken off in one of the smuggling brigs —armed vessels they were—that plied between our coast and the Channel Islands.

Any way, there was great fright and confusion when the fire spread, that was caused by one of the men who sat up late, waiting for my lord, leaving a candle burning in the new harness-room. It was not got under till the flames reached the fine picture-gallery, and destroyed the cases, not yet unpacked, which had been sent over from Italy. His Lordship, who was then a very strong, active man, worked as hard as any one to save his property.

"All that part of the building which had been the old chapel was burnt, and Madame's oratory, where she went to do penance and talk to the priest. It lies in ruins; but yonder, over the archway, is the little closet where she used to dress herself; and chests full of her fine clothes are mouldering away there now; French silks and satins, some of them as good as new; and there are her fans and pomander box, and her little high-heeled shoes, fit for a fairy.

"That night, while the place was still in a blaze from the fire, which has left its marks to this day on some of the great oaks and beeches, my mother, who was still-room-maid, saw the foreign lady, dressed in black, with her baby in her arms, come down the great staircase, and through the hall, crying bitterly, just as foolish people say she often passes by;

but I never saw her. She let herself out into the woods, and no living person, to my knowledge, ever saw her again.

"When mother told what she had seen, people always said it must have been the lady's ghost, but she never believed it. My lord did not stay here long; he went away, and only came back once, when nothing seemed to please him. I mind that visit myself, and how scared I used to be with the tales about the house being haunted. He laughed at first, and then grew angry, and moved from room to room; but, whether he saw anything more than common, no mortal but himself could tell. When he went away he gave his cousin, Captain Fleming, leave to bide at the Grange, and much good he hoped it would do him. Master had married, and wanted a house to live in; so he took my lord at his word: but the place brought him ill-luck. After his death, people talked more than ever about the ghosts, and mixed up the old tales about my lord and the French lady, and my poor master's being made away with, till folks could not sleep in their beds for terror; and so it has been ever since. I am afraid there have been bad deeds done here, and not repented of as they ought to be; but if you've a clear conscience, you may live at 'Oods comfortably enough, as I have done, and never saw anything supernatural, all through the darkest night, summer or winter."

The woman gathered up the savoury herbs in her apron, and went in-doors; while Reine, who had let her work drop into her lap as she listened to Leah's garrulous talk, remained with her eyes dreamily fixed on the masses of waving foliage, and with thoughts that wandered from the gloomy mansion before her, to pleasanter ideas connected with the breezy woodland.

Trotting along the mossy path, which led past the gate of the orchard, there came presently, on his donkey, the old man whom Reine had seen in charge of the run of water near the ruined church in the hollow of the down. He rode on, peering about as if in search of somebody, and stopped by the side of the wall where it was broken away. Then he went a little farther, and came to a standstill at the entrance of the enclosure, nodding his head and making signs to the young girl, as if he wished to speak to her.

Reine was too good-natured not to indulge him. She went to the gate, and asked if she should call Mrs. Scriven, or any one else, to hear what he wanted.

" Be you the pretty ma'amselle down to 'Oods?" inquired the old man, mysteriously pointing with his thumb to the corner of the grey house visible through the trees. "You speak terrible fine English—be you hur, I say?"

"Yes!" said Reine, laughing. "I came from France last month. Is your errand to me?"

"Surely," answered her quaint interlocutor, sitting easily on his donkey, after kicking it to make it draw closer up to the gate. "You be just like hur, for certain. Didn't I see ye once with Helier's girls, them skittish creatures that never go past without casting sticks and stones to trouble the watercourse? They should learn better manners from ye. Well, if you be the French young lady with the dark hair and eyes that came in the schooner, I'm thinking I've got a message for ye. Do you know any gentleman that's staying at Lezant town?—not the church town, mind ye, but down by the water-side —at the Boscawen Arms? Would you like to know where he is to be found?—where he's looking for you to meet him, this evening?"

Reine hesitated. She did not quite like the aspect of the cunning old fellow, as he sat, with his eyes twinkling, watching her keenly; but she felt a great desire to know where Richard was, and whether he were really expecting her.

"I owe ye a good turn," said the old man. "I be poor, but honest; and the Lieutenant paid me for doing a bit of work that didn't answer. Some way or other, I lost his note: I suppose, while I was looking after the water. You didn't ever happen to get. it, did ye?"

"Yes," said Reine, taken by surprise; "but too late to be of use. Are you sure that the same person bade you speak to me now?"

"Well, he didn't exactly say it in so many words; but he's waiting for ye—that is, he will be by then ye get there—up among the hills, where ye went once with the children. But you'd best not trouble to take them along with ye. They make more work than enough with their mischievous hands, and won't ever let the runlet be. The Lieutenant's going up to the old church at sundown; I can tell ye that; and he'll be sore angry if there's nought there but the tombstones that once had a brave lot of brandy under them; but, most ways, only corpses. It's not a good place for him to bide in after dark. There's the Gauger's Hole stopped with a slate slab, not far off over the moor, and few honest folk passing. You'd best not keep him waiting."

He gave his beast a kick and a smart

stroke with his cudgel, and rode on, leaving
Reine far from certain of his trustworthiness,
but unable to guess what motive he could
have for deceiving her. She did not look for
the young girls to be her companions ; but,
after waiting till the old man was out of sight,
she tied down her bonnet closely, and took her
way to the ruined chapel on the moor.

Though the walk was lonely, she was not
afraid of it, and she knew the road perfectly.
In fact, the stream would have guided her,
and she heard it rippling as she went sometimes along its bank ; at others, crossing
wide stretches of turf, and coming back to
the water. Though the sun was declining,
it was not yet near its setting, and she walked
slowly, gathering the blue harebells that
nodded on the hillocks, and stopping frequently to look around her.

When she came to the angle of the churchyard wall which inclosed Fleming's grave,
where the brook rippled among the flags, and
gushed with a mournful rhythm over the
broken fragments of stone that had fallen
into the water and impeded its course, Reine
paused to survey the spot with more interest
than it had previously excited. The young
Helier girls had pointed to it shudderingly,
as the grave of the murdered man whose
ghost still walked at Woods.. Reine had not

wished, then, to approach more closely; but now she went straight thither, upon entering the enclosure; making her way, not without difficulty, through the weeds and rubbish with which the neglected, solitary burial-ground was encumbered.

The impressionable French girl's eyes filled with tears as she looked at the low headstone, with merely a name and date recorded upon it; and thought of the misery which had been caused to many by the event that lonely tomb brought to her recollection. She understood, now, Richard's allusion to his own darkened prospects, and the obscurity which he shrank from inviting her to share. She could not accustom herself to the idea of his new name; for so it appeared to her, as she whispered it softly. Low as her tone was, she fancied that the murmuring flags, the gushing, melancholy flow of the water, repeated the sound.

Reine rose up quickly, and went to the other side of the church, where she could see the sun going down upon the moor. The long, sweeping lines of the distant prospect were softened by the slanting gleams which, far away, where the land fell lower, sparkled and glittered on the western sea. She could trace the path she had pursued, winding by the side of the brook, and the dark hollow formed by the wooded ravine. The light passed off the summit of the heights, though she still saw a golden gleam upon the ocean. She had waited nearly an hour, and the chill of disappointed feelings was beginning to creep over her, when a man's figure came in front of the trees in the hollow. She watched it pass the different windings of the stream and cross the turf, cutting off every unnecessary angle, till it reached the corner of the church-yard wall where she had rested for a few moments. Then she rose from her seat: the next instant, Richard St. Erme was standing beside her.

Reine did not struggle with the tender, compassionate feelings which, while she waited for his coming, had filled her heart. She allowed him to draw her towards him; and, for the first time, he passed his arm round her slender waist. He saw that she had ceased to doubt or to misjudge him, before they had interchanged a word with each other.

" I scarcely hoped to find you here, Reine; but the old man, for once, told me truth," said the young officer, as they sat down to-gether on some fragments of stone under the window of the church. " He shall not go unrewarded; nevertheless, I would not have you trust him in general. What became of the note I once confided to him for you? I believe that it gave information to the smugglers, of which they made good use."

"Certainly it did not reach my hands through any channel you had chosen," said Reine. "One of the little girls at Woods took it from her brother, who was teasing her to translate it for him, and she threw it into the waterfall. Bouffe, the dog that came over with me from France, thought that it was mine, and brought it to me."

"He shall have a silver collar, with the date and circumstance engraven upon it to his honour," said Osborne, laughing. "Truly, Reine, the dog is your most respectable companion. I have every reason to believe this meeting with you to-night among the hills to be a trap laid for me by your precious friends at Woods, and their associates at Lezant, who contemplate availing themselves of my absence to regain possession of the smuggled goods. Only, this time they have reckoned without their host."

"Ciel! que tu es téméraire? Your life is not safe an hour from those men who are so angry," said Reine, shivering. "On the cliff, coming from Arthur's Castle, you were beset, and would, perhaps, have been murdered, but for Mademoiselle St. Erme's protection. Oh, Richard, I shall always love her for saving

you — now that I know she is your sister," she
added, with a blush and a smile. " But tell
me — what have you done with the goods?
Ah, you must not return to Lezant. Is the
Curlew off the coast?"

" No," answered Richard. " Her movements are retarded by this adverse wind; but
there was in the port a collier brig. No one
suspected our intention. A strong guard,
night and day, kept the people of Lezant from
approaching the storehouses, while their contents were privately removed and carried on
board the collier, which lifted her anchor and
sailed out of the harbour at two o'clock to-day.
My men all quitted the place before me. All
I regret in leaving that abominable town is,
that I shall not see the mortified faces of the
rogues who were determined to break open
the stores to-night, when they learn, as they will
do in time to prevent mischief, that they are
empty. Every cask and bale dug up in Dame
Brock's garden is on its way to Bristol."

He looked so happy and triumphant that
Reine's fears passed away, and she joined in
the laugh with him. The old deserted ruin,
the murmuring rivulet as it wound among the
weeds and gravestones, had lost their usual
lugubrious aspect. The falling water, the
rustling flags and fern-leaves, sighed pleasantly
in the evening breeze.

"Reine," said Richard, after a brief silence, " you know me now—the stigma which rests upon my name, and made me—unwillingly indeed—consent to lay it aside: all this, I care not how, has been revealed to you. I am glad that it is so. Now, tell me—these gloomy prospects, this obscurity, are they too terrible for you to risk involving yourself. in my darkened fortunes? Must I lay aside even the hope that, when a brighter day dawns, you will share in its prosperity, even as you have taken part in my early troubles? You were the first, though you did not know their origin, to soothe them."

Reine looked at him with eyes blinded by tears. "Ah, it is I who am obscure," she said. "Your friends would never consent to our union. You are under a cloud, now; but it will pass off: while I, to my life's end, I shall be but the daughter of the Breton trader. It may be," she said, tremulously, "that in his own dwelling-place, where he was known, we were respected. You, in your lone childhood, found our house among the vineyards a pleasant home; but, we are not of the same class. You will think differently, when you have been long in England, from what you now do, when all things wear a strange, and for the present, an unfavourable aspect. I

will not let you pledge yourself to that which
you might hereafter repent."

"Not so—on my life, my honour!" said
Richard, with much agitation. "Reine, if I
win myself a name, as I intend to do, my
chief spur to exertion must be your love. See!
this is not a cheerful trysting-place; but here,
with the dead resting in their graves around
us, I swear to you solemnly that no other
woman shall ever be my wife. Will you not
say as much, Reine? Could either of us love
another?"

Whether the one soft word that rose to
her lips was in French or English, Richard
understood it. Reine stood up immediately.

"We must part now," she said, hurriedly.
"The sunlight is gone quite off the sea.
Where are you going to-night? Not to
Lezant, I trust? Your life would be in
peril."

"My road lies yonder," said Richard,
pointing along the track which wound past
the church, over the moor. "But I must see
you home first."

"No!" said Reine, decidedly. "I will
never say one word of kindness to you again,
if you go one step with me of the path that
leads to Lezant. What should harm me? It
is not dark, though the sun has set; and

I—I am not fearful. Now, go; you have a long, dreary road before you, but I would rather think of you travelling alone with the stars to light you, than in that bad town, with its idle, lawless people."

He walked by her side for a few moments, but she would not allow him to go farther than the gate leading out of the churchyard. He stood with his arms folded, watching her as she went swiftly and steadily on her way in the twilight, with the brawling stream to keep her company; and then he turned off, crossing the moor with a quick, manly tread, that carried him in an hour's time to the road-side inn, four miles from Lezant, by which the night-coach passed on its way from Camelford to Exeter.

CHAPTER XIII.

THE inmates of the houses in the main street at Lezant looked out with surprise, as Simon Brock, the infirm landlord of the Three Crowns, walked slowly and painfully, stick in hand, past their different dwellings. Several persons spoke to him, and the old man, probably glad of a halt now and then, and always quiet and civil, responded to their inquiries after his health by saying he was better than he had felt for many a day, and was going to have a look at the harbour and the new buildings. He did not refuse a helping hand when it was offered by one of his neighbours, more inquisitive or more good-natured than the rest; but the rough, steep bit of irregular paving once passed over, he let go his friend's arm, thanking him, and saying he could get along by himself now.

There were not many people about on the quay. No vessels had entered the port lately, and it was the workmen's dinner-hour. The old publican stood for a few minutes by the water-side, counting the boats, and watching the waves as they broke against the sea-wall close under his feet. Then he turned about, and walked, with his usual feeble, halting gait, but deliberately, as if acting on a pre-conceived intention, across the road to the Boscawen Arms.

The door of the new inn was shut. It did not usually stand open, like the portal of the old village hostelry. Simon Brock knocked with the end of his walking-stick against the oak panel, and obtained entrance immediately. He did not take any notice of the pretty, fair-haired child who stood, half-frightened, holding the door ajar, but strode, with steps that still sounded manly, across the flagged passage into the tap-room, stooping his head as he entered, more from habit than necessity. Time had been when Simon Brock could not have gone into any house in Lezant town, if he carried himself perfectly upright.

Morgan Price's pretty, delicate wife, paler than usual, and with a shawl wrapped about her, was sitting in the bar, talking to a tall, angular-looking personage, who turned round sharply at the sound of footsteps in the passage. The young woman was struck with the old man's venerable appearance, and set a chair for him, asking what he would be pleased to take. She did not know him in

the least; it was many a year since he had
been so far from his own fireside, and there
she was not likely to have seen him.

The person with whom she was speaking
stared at the old innkeeper, while Simon
Brock fumbled in his pocket for change, and
ordered a hot drink, which was prepared for
him immediately, and set attentively on a little
table near the fire, and close at his elbow.
The weariness he felt was excessive after his
long walk. He sat down, sighing, and me-
chanically lighted his pipe, puffing away, and
watching the smoke ascend, or knocking the
ashes from the bowl, as he bent towards the
flame without speaking, his withered, but
clear-complexioned face brightening in the
warm glow.

"Good morning, Mr. Brock!" said the
stranger, suddenly, while Mrs. Price flushed
up to her thin temples at the sound of that
name; "it is a good step from your house: I
scarcely expected to see you here. Is the
Dame well? She keeps hearty, I am told,
and does not afford much help to the faculty.
Shall I give her a call as I pass by?"

"She's well enough; nothing ever ails
her," said the old man, looking up. "I
beg your pardon, Sir, but I'm mortal tired.
I've not been on my legs so long these
eighteen year. You be the doctor from

Camelford, that told me it would be next door to a miracle if I ever set foot to the ground again."

"Did I?" said the surgeon, laughing. "Well, I am glad you have falsified my prophecy. It was a bad case, though — compound fracture; wonderful every bone in your skin was not broken. I thought it was, at first. The case is down in my books; and a capital cure I made of it. A little infirm: but what could you expect after such a fall? You've not been out on the cliffs stargazing of late, I fancy."

He laughed again. Mrs. Price looked compassionately at the still handsome, but, as she now perceived, disabled figure of the rival publican. He took the glass she gave him with his left hand, the right arm and side having become paralysed, after the severe accident he had met with.

"No, no!" he said, with a groan; "that was the last time. I have scarcely been out of my house since; and I'm not master there. Things don't go on as I like to have them, but it's of no use complaining; my dame works hard and she chooses to have her own way, and I can't hinder her. I never get such a comforting glass as this, though other folks say our tap's a good one; but nought tastes good that's served to you grudgingly. It's a hard lot to bear; a rancorous tongue is the worst of company."

He set the glass down, and again sat looking into the fire. The Doctor turned towards his patient.

"We shall have you ill again," he said, "if you bustle about too much. When will your husband be at home?"

"Oh, not yet awhile," answered the young wife, with manifest anxiety. "He's gone on business to Swansea, and I told him 'twas best not to hurry it over; he'll maybe not come back this fortnight."

"Tell him the longer he can make it last out the better!" said Simon Brock, turning towards her. "There are men in this place that have bound themselves to kill him, as the wicked Jews were banded together to murder the blessed Apostle. The word has gone out, I tell you, and he's not safe in this town, neither by day nor yet by night; you'd best send him word to keep away."

"Come, come! this must be exaggerated," said the surgeon, seeing Mrs. Price turn deadly pale at the warning. "You must tell your customers at the Three Crowns, my master, not to carry the joke too far; the law can reach into the remotest corner of civilised England. We must not have murder plotted in broad daylight, even in Lezant. Do you mean to say that a man who neither meddles nor makes—who pays rates and tithes and taxes honestly—cannot carry on his lawful traffic in your town without being in peril of his life?"

"That's the question, Sir. It's differently answered according as you put it. I've heard men say that Morgan Price did meddle and make, and was an acting partner in the bales and tubs being carried off by sea, that never would have left this place by land. Yes, and that he got a profit by it, which is to be laid out in the goods he's bringing back with him."

"Indeed, my husband had no share in shipping the Custom-house property that lay in the stores by the water-side," exclaimed Mrs. Price, in great alarm. "The Swansea brig was only waiting for a wind in the harbour. I can't think why the people in this place are so set against us. As Dr. Lawrence says, we keep to our business, and desire to have nothing to do with them. I wish they minded their own affairs, and would let us alone!"

The poor young woman burst into tears. Her situation in this unfriendly town was, at present, lonely and unprotected enough; yet she dreaded, more than she could express, her husband's return. She got up, and busied herself in dusting the tumblers and mugs, striving to disguise her emotion.

"Who is the young officer that has been

staying with you?" said the surgeon. "I have heard strange reports about him to-day. Is it true that he is the nephew of your old clergyman—a son, in fact, of the banished man, Colonel St. Erme?"

"I'm sure, Sir, I don't know; it's no business of mine," said the young, timid hostess. "Since I've kept this inn, I've taken care to ask no questions. He's a gentleman, and a kind, good one, that would not have said a word or done a deed that should bring us into such trouble. He slept here, and dined, and so forth, and paid for what he had; but Price had nothing to do with the removal of the stores. They were carried down, I believe, by the seamen belonging to the cutter, and put on board the smack that sailed last week; at least, so I heard, but he never mentioned it. Morgan did not lift a hand from first to last, and knows no more about the people of this place than the child yonder. I wish with all my heart we had never come here!"

"A son of Colonel St. Erme?" said the old man, who had not heard a word she uttered, so intently had he been pondering over the last words pronounced in clear, emphatic tones by the surgeon. "That would make him brother to Miss Mary: I mind her father well."

"Do you, my old friend?" said the

medical man. "That ugly fall you got just at the time of his trial has not unsettled your memory, then, altogether; and yet, from my experience in cases like yours, I should suppose that, while long-past events might stand out clear and unforgotten, those occurring at the time, or near about the period of your accident, would be vague and indistinct."

"I mind the Colonel well, I tell ye," persisted the old man; "better, much better, than folks I have seen since. He was a fine soldierly man; but he always said, 'Brock! you 're half a head taller than I am.' That's what I mind most about him."

"Well, well! there's not much in that," said Mr. Lawrence, laughing. "He might have said you would have been a capital grenadier in that regiment of the King of Prussia's, in which giants only were enrolled. Colonel St. Erme was a fine-looking man. I saw him at his trial, and those who did so are not likely to forget it. To see a soldier, and a brave one—a gentleman, and such a perfect gentleman — stand in dock accused of a heinous crime, was a remarkable event. I have more than one memento of that day in my museum at Camelford."

"Sure, Sir! you can't think he was guilty?" said Mrs. Price, who had by this time somewhat recovered herself. "Not if

the Lieutenant is his son, and like him, as they
say. Why, my boys were not afraid of him,
and they 're the timidest little creatures! He
wouldn't hurt a fly."

"Can't say, Mrs. Price! can't say! For-
tunately I am not called upon to pronounce
judgment in this case, which has been long
since decided. There was very strong
evidence against the Colonel, chiefly, however, if I recollect rightly, of a circumstantial
kind. The probabilities founded upon his
high birth and general character were certainly in his favour. So, this young officer is
said to be like him? Has he left Lezant?
I am sorry I did not make his acquaintance."

"Yes, Sir; he went away a week ago,"
answered Mrs. Price. "I have heard that he
got great credit for seizing the smuggling
schooner's cargo, and sending it off without
bloodshed; but the men of Lezant never will
forgive him, nor any one else they choose
in their wicked hearts to think had a share in
this matter. My husband left the morning
before, little guessing what trouble I should
be in, and I do not wish him to know it. I
am not much afraid for myself and the little
ones. Bad as they are, sure the people won't
harm women and children; but this good
man is right in thinking, if they have a spite

against Morgan, his life would not be safe till this ill-wind has blown over."

" Well, I don't think you are fit to be left alone. Shall I speak to the officer of the Customs at Camelford, or the magistrates at the Town-hall, on Friday ? It is their duty to protect you," said the Doctor, drawing on his gloves and preparing to depart. " Mr. Brock has done a good deed in giving you this warning ; but I should like to inquire a little more particularly into the nature of the danger. What is it these bad subjects have in contemplation ? "

He faced round as he spoke, and confronted the old man, who was smoking his pipe dreamily over the fire.

" Nay, I 've told ye enough, I think ! " answered the landlord of the Three Crowns. " There 's a set of them banded together, and I can tell ye, they think little of murder when it comes in their way. Why, but for Miss Mary, they would have hustled the Lieutenant off the cliff! I mind the place—it 's not far off where I fell, and much steeper. He 'd have gone down where there 's nought but the gulls and puffins to heed his cries. I mind them screeching. It has rung in my ears o' nights often since."

" So! this is news to me ! " said the surgeon, reseating himself and drawing his chair nearer. "These neighbours of yours tried to murder the young officer belonging to the Revenue vessel, and Miss St. Erme saved him? How did she manage that?"

"I never heard them say what she did, exactly," replied Simon Brock, thoughtfully. "There's a charm of holiness about her that stops their wicked talk; and I suppose she heard the men cursing and swearing outside the Parsonage shrubberies, and went to hinder them from committing mischief. If it was as you say, and the Lieutenant was her own brother, Heaven put it in her heart to look for him. I've not heard of it from herself; she has not been at my house lately, and the folks that come there are wickeder than ever. I waited and waited, after I heard them threatening this person and that, till at last I was forced to go and give this bit of warning. So now, dame, good-bye to ye."

The young woman thanked him, with tears in her eyes, for the trouble he had taken. She picked up his stick, and saw him to the door, watching his slow progress up the street for some moments before she came back to her seat within the bar.

"That's a curious old fellow!" said Doctor Lawrence. "But he has done you a good turn, probably at some cost to himself. I don't envy him his reception when he gets

home. Now say, is there anything I can do
for you? Time runs on, and I must keep
moving. I shall see you again shortly."

The young landlady declined his offer to
represent her case to the local authorities.
"I don't think there is any real danger for
me, Sir; and I wouldn't wish to incur more ·
ill-will if I can help it. Price need never
know how unwell I have been, now that I am
about again; and I shall write to urge his
staying away till the end of the month. He
is amongst his own people, and will like it.
By that time, it is to be hoped, those wicked
hill-folk will have got some other piece of
mischief in their heads. Perhaps the French
schooner may be back."

"Ah, by the way, that is what I wanted
to know!" said the surgeon, turning round
just as he got to the door. "Is that really
Jacob Mohr's vessel — the famous Dutch
skipper? I wish to Heaven he would bring
me some tulips. I hear he has the choicest
cigars, spices, and coffee, and has picked up
some curious bits of china and Japan-work.
The man, in his way, is a perfect *virtuoso*.
Not, of course, that a sober citizen like myself would have dealings with such a character.
But have you any idea when his friends at
Lezant expect to see him again?"

"Indeed, Sir, I cannot tell you," said Mrs.

Price gravely. " It was only an idle word of mine, that he might be on his way over, and so give the people here something to think about, instead of harming us in our business. Lieutenant Osborne and the cutter people put up here at the Boscawen; *we* have no dealings with the smugglers. Their inn is the Three Crowns. Dame Brock might tell you what you wish to know. It is no affair of ours."

" To be sure! to be sure! quite right! of course not," answered the Doctor. " It 's not of the slightest consequence. I only asked from mere curiosity. Look here, now! if you should be in any fresh trouble, just send for me; I shan't mind the ride, and there 's generally something worth noting in these popular tumults. In particular, if that young Lieutenant should come here again, oblige me by letting me know. I remember some curious particulars about his father's trial; and, in short, it is my hobby to like to know a little of every stranger that comes into my beat. I am nearly sure I saw this young fellow on the top of the coach the other day; a likeness struck me, but I could not put the face and the facts brought to my mind together. I should like to see him again."

Mrs. Price promised very readily to comply with this request; and the Doctor, hur-

rying off with alacrity, was soon riding his
strong bony horse, not unlike himself in the
build, up the steep street of Lezant. He
passed old Simon Brock proceeding very
slowly on his homeward way; and nodded
familiarly to Dame Brock, as she stood at
the door of the Three Crowns, with an
ominous frown upon her brow, looking out
for her husband. Dr. Lawrence, whose discretion, in spite of his boundless curiosity, was
unimpeachable, did not slacken his pace to
speak to her. He felt by no means inclined
to inform the irascible matron, in whose company and underneath what roof he had lately
beheld old Simon.

He rode swiftly over the moors in the
direction of his native town, where he had
resided during the greater part of his life, and
now, having risen to some eminence in his
profession, possessed one of the best houses
in the place. It was a wild and barren ride,
over green turf strewn with fragments of
granite—Brown Willy and Row Tor rising
above the bold, free expanse through which
wind the Fowey and the Camel; but the
Doctor enjoyed it, and would have felt cooped
up in a thickly-planted, cultivated country.
No one was better acquainted with the pecu-
liarities of the scenery and the habits of the
country-people than Dr. Lawrence, as they

called him, though he had never taken out
his diploma. In his own odd way he was
a man of extensive information, and of some
scientific tastes and acquirements.

He had a large practice, principally among
the miners, and many a dark tragedy in those
wild and lawless districts had probably come
to his knowledge. Nothing would be said by
him about such cases to any living mortal,
but he never rested till he came to the bottom
of them. He had a way of asking shrewd
questions, fitter, perhaps, for a lawyer than
a physician; but, if his patients unguardedly
betrayed more than was prudent, such revela-
tions were sacred. He locked them up in
the strong chest of his memory, and never let
them escape him; nay, he would take infinite
trouble to sift collateral facts, which might
have furnished important evidence in a court
of justice: but he made no use of them. Like
the stores of quaint objects which garnished
the shelves of his museum at Camelford, these
miscellaneous pieces of information, when once
collected by him, were generally valueless,
except to himself.

He had also in his recollection a vast mass
of anecdotes and details respecting former
patients and their maladies, with which, by
way of elucidating his plan of treatment, he
occasionally entertained those who needed his

services. In his gallery might be seen ana-
tomical subjects of the most unpleasing kind,
recalling to him operations skilfully performed;
but from these his visitors generally turned
away. There were, besides, exceedingly rare
and interesting specimens of ores and fossils,
botanical curiosities, and antiquarian and other
relics, to each of which — in the Doctor's eye
and mind at least — was attached a legend of
the past or a story of more recent times,
which made him treasure them.

CHAPTER XIV.

OUTSIDE the small but ancient borough of Camelford — now disfranchised, but which never, in its most prosperous days, included more than a hundred houses — there stood, among dreary hills, verging on the moor, a solitary dwelling. A few fields, indifferently cultivated, lay around, constituting a small copyhold farm ; of which possession had lately been taken, after paying the usual fees to the lord of the manor, by persons little known in the country. These people did not attend church, fair, or market. The first, indeed, was almost impossible, so considerable was the distance from Lanteglos, the parish-church of Camelford, which lay on the other side of the town. The produce of the land was said to be disposed of to the foreign traders who put into the ports along the coast, and brought in return supplies of various kinds for the use of the family.

There was very little appearance of comfort about the place. The stone walls looked cold and bare, and the few trees growing in the enclosure, though sheltered in some measure by the house, were scathed and twisted by the blast. A rough bridle-road passed close under the palings in front, and wound away over the granitic district which extended for miles around—the very barrenness of desolation. Broods of geese cackled and swam about marshy, reed-covered ponds near the dwelling; while in the far distance Row Tor and Brown Willy showed their majestic russet summits over the grey expanse of the moorland.

At the door of this unpromising dwelling the Doctor, whose practice carried him everywhere, knocked for admission, on the afternoon of the same day on which he visited Lezant. A man's voice, subdued in tone, probably by sickness, bade him enter. He seemed to know his way; and passing the doors, on either hand, of kitchen and parlour which opened into the passage, Mr. Lawrence went on to a room at the back, looking into a plot of ground planted with cabbages and potatoes, at the bottom of which flowed the Camel—here but a shallow stream, rising in a neighbouring hamlet; whence the " crooked river," whose waters, according to tradition, once ran red with the blood of Arthur and his bravest warriors, wound its way to the sea.

The face of the man sitting at the window

of the inner room brightened at the sound of approaching footsteps. " Come in!" he said again, impatiently, as the Doctor paused for a moment at the door. " There's nothing to hinder you, and you 're sure not to interrupt me. When shall I be up, and stirring again, Sir? This shore life doesn't suit me."

" Well, you had better not be in too great a hurry," said the Doctor, with professional caution, sitting down and feeling the pulse that still beat feebly in the brawny wrist held out to him. " Such a fever as we have brought you through leaves its traces behind for some time. I assure you we may consider ourselves fortunate to have escaped so well. Has anybody caught the infection?"

" No, no! not a soul in the house has sickened. Faugh, I wonder at it! Those dismal pools are enough to gender fevers. There's always foul air creeping over them, and the cackle of those confounded geese a'most drives me mad. I'd give more than the pay I am likely to get for the next six months to be afloat again. Have you heard anything, sir," he added, lowering his tone, " of our schooner?"

" She's not expected back yet awhile. You must have patience. This place seems safe and quiet, though certainly not the cheerfullest I ever saw ; still, it has its recommendations.

You can creep out when your strength returns, and walk about a bit, without much danger of falling in with more company than you like. I thought you might have heard from Mynheer."

" Not I ! " answered the mate of La Belle Marie, sullenly. " I don't believe the letters come safe through that post-office at Camelford. News gets abroad that is told only under seal and cover ; and I ought to have had word of the schooner by this time. There are sharp eyes on the watch, and money changing hands, too. I can tell you there is better guard kept than formerly. You didn't mention to anybody," he inquired, anxiously, " who it was you were coming to see?"

" My friend, I have lived long enough in the world to learn the truth of the old adage, '. Least said, soonest mended ;' especially as regards professional visits. My practice, as you well know, places me by the bedsides of men — sick, perhaps dying — who cannot keep guard over their lips. Secrets have been revealed to me, alike in the houses of great men and in wild cabins among the hills, touching upon matters of life and death — yes, and worth gold, too ; since large sums have been offered for them ; but these will die with me. Depend upon it, if there is, as gossips say, a skeleton in every house,

the doctor, in most cases, knows where to
look for it!"

"I believe you," said the sailor. "You
must have heard some curious things in your
time; and I never knew of your blabbing.
It's a comfort to meet with an honest
man, that can hold his tongue, once in a
way.

"So, honesty is your motto!" said the
surgeon. "For my part, I think most men
love roguery and mischief in some form or
other, and would rather, at any risk, get what
they want from the contraband trader, than
as good an article, at a fair price, at the shop
in the village. That is why we all look out
for La Belle Marie and her unlawful cargo.
I have a hankering, I confess, for those choice
cigars you told me Mynheer was to bring
over; and a tulip is the only flower I care
for. The Havannahs might lie hid under the
bulbs. Where is the skipper now?"

"It's difficult to say exactly," answered
the mate, cautiously. "Let's talk of something else. How should I know, cooped up
as I am within four walls? If one could only
have a whiff of the salt breeze, or a sight of
the blue water! — but I've scarce breath to
fill my sails in this cranny among the hills.
Can't you set a craft to rights a bit quicker?
By the time you've been caulking the seams

and trimming the sails it ought to be out of harbour."

" Come, come! that was an uncommonly ugly attack you called me in for. Don't be ungrateful! You are a different man from when I first saw you—lightheaded with fever, and had to take more blood from you than a man sheds willingly, even in the best of causes. It is a sure sign you are getting better when you become impatient. I dare say, if truth were told, you never were ill ten days in your whole life before; and, instead of acknowledging this exemption with thankfulness, you are ready to run your head against a stone wall the first time such a calamity overtakes you. By-the-bye, now you are in your right senses, have you any notion what brought on the complaint? What had you been doing with yourself on shore? Had you been drinking? I should judge you to be a sober fellow, in general."

" Hang me, if I don't think it was the air of the haunted house that disagreed with me!" said the sailor. " I don't mind telling *you* that we—that is, Mynheer and I— had been up to Woods with Lance Fleming. The skipper took it into his head to sleep there, and sent me back, before daybreak, to the schooner, to tell the boat's crew to pull in and take him off the quay at Lezant, by

five o'clock in the morning. Well! it was
dark enough when I started, and colder than
I almost ever remember it; or else the shiver-
ings were coming upon me. I hauled up,
more than once, and made a fresh tack, before I got clear of the bushes. I was wet and
tired when I got on board and turned in;
but what bothered me most was seeing people
come about my berth that I had not set eyes
on for years till that night — fellows that were
friends, too, once. I suppose it must have
been my coming across the Jerseyman — Mr.
Helier, as they call him here — that conjured
up such queer fancies."

"Helier of Woods? So, you and he
were allies once?" said the surgeon. "How
did that come to pass? No one in this part
of the country is acquainted with his ante-
cedents. Where did you fall in with each
other?"

"Why, when I was a lad, there was a
brisk trade carried on along the Sussex coast,
and where I was reared, down to Hurstmon-
ceaux. Most of us had dealings with the
French Brothers, Jean and Gervase Helier.
Jerseymen they professed to be; but, besides
their lingo, there was a foreign look about
their black muzzles. That poor, chicken-
hearted fellow, trembling at his own shadow
in the moonlight, was a perfect terror to the

Excise. Whatever he said he would do, that
he did; aye, and did it well, too! I'll be
bound they tell of his daring deeds yet at
Rotherbridge, and down by the yew-trees in
Kingley Bottom! 'Twas there he courted
Phœbe Bower, daughter of one of the Duke's
farmers, the prettiest girl in all the country
round. I've seen them together, making
love in the vale, when the morning sun
wasn't high enough to dry the dew on the
grass; across which the dainty lass stole,
while her old father was asleep, to meet her
smuggling lover!"

"Bower?" said Mr. Lawrence, sharply.
"That was Mrs. Fleming's maiden name. I
did not know that she and her second husband were such old acquaintances."

"Like enough not. Jean was a close
chap, and Mistress Fleming might not be
over-fond of talking of her old sweetheart,"
said the mate. "Her father, old Archdale
Bower, made short work of their wooing, for
he was a thorough Englishman, and hated all
foreigners. He locked Miss Phœbe up, and
spliced her out of hand—with a pretty fortune, too!—to a young soldier-officer quar-
tered at Chichester. Savage Jack was away
on one of his trips; and the farmer, who was
rich enough to purchase the lugger ten times
over, swore he'd lay his daughter—and she

was the only child he had — in churchyard mould, sooner than she should marry the fellow. Jean was sorely beneath her; but he had a way with him that wiled the heart out of a woman's bosom. Some said, it was more through fear than fondness. Gervase was a different man — frank, and free, and pleasant-spoken. I've known him dancing the night through at fairs and wakes, when a hundred pounds was set on his head; but they nabbed him at last off Pevensey, after a hard fight, and he was shipped off for the Colonies.

" There's nothing doing now, compared to the business that was carried on in those days by the great Sussex smugglers!" continued the mate. " Those deep-wooded valleys, with hills that were almost mountains, and close-banked lanes running down to the coast, were famous places. Then, the shore was, generally speaking, more open, and we knew how to manage to run a cargo upon it and beach a boat on the shingle in the wildest weather. Few could beat us at that! As for the Excisemen, we laughed at them, and carried the goods away before their eyes. It was seldom they ventured to interfere with us; and if it came to a hand-to-hand fight, ten to one we got off the best. Now and then, the military were called in, or one of the King's cutters would land a boat-load or two of seamen ; but most of the country-people were on our side, and we generally left our mark behind us, even if we were forced to abandon our cargo."

" What could have changed this man Helier's nature so completely ?　He is of quite a different constitution now," said the Doctor, thoughtfully.　" He is seldom seen beyond his own premises, and he goes about his farm with his eyes on the ground—cheated, so it is said, by his own people as well as strangers. It is a wonder Lord Boscawen's steward has not displaced him.　I thought your Captain's colleagues were men 'of a different stamp— dare-devils, like Lance Fleming ? "

" Jean Helier's name is the first on the list now," said the mate of La Belle Marie, pulling from his pocket a folded paper.　" There are the addresses of those with whom I am to communicate freely.　Mynheer wrote it him- self at Woods.　Part of our next cargo—the most valuable half, too—is consigned to him. I don't half like it.　When once such a man loses heart, his whole character changes—he is as likely as not to turn informer.　I scarce knew him, groping about in the dark—bent double like an old man—scared at our foot- steps."

Mr. Lawrence looked curiously at the paper, which the seaman held tight in his grasp.　" I would not risk much on any venture in which Jean Helier had a share. He is a slippery fellow — a coward, perhaps a knave. I wonder Captain Mohr trusts him."

"Oh, for that matter, Mynheer has his secrets; but I made out that it was not the first time they had been concerned together. Jacob Mohr seemed quite at his ease in the old house. Helier and he were like brothers —yes, that was what he said that night when he woke me up to send me back to the boat, and I tried to put in a word for Lance Fleming, who would not be best pleased at our having dealings with his step-father."

"Brothers!" said Mr. Lawrence, quickly. "Are you sure that was Captain Mohr's expression? That is a remarkable word."

"Aye, aye! — that was it — you may put it down in the log-book," said the mate, laughing, as Mr. Lawrence made a hasty note in his pocket-book. "If I wanted to pick a brother out of the lot, hang me if it should be Savage Jack! But that was our skipper's foreign way of speaking. Perhaps it did not mean quite as much as brotherhood does in English."

"This man's brother—Gervase Helier, I mean, the Sussex smuggler who was transported — did he never come back?" asked the surgeon, after finishing his memorandum, still holding the pencil in his hand. "How many years is it since you saw him?"

"Nigh upon twenty," answered the mate. "For aught I know, he may be dead long since, or changed past recollection. I'm not sure, if it had not been for the name, that I should have minded Jean Helier's face when he first came across me. I was but a lad in those brisk days, and the old place at home got too hot to hold me; so, sooner than be sent to serve in a King's ship for three years, in the war time, I slung my hammock on board a South-Sea whaler, and didn't come back to England till the scent had got cold. I've been knocking about the high seas since, off and on, till Mynheer took a fancy to the cut of my jib, and offered me a berth on board the schooner; and I've never tired of the bargain till I found myself laid up, high and dry, on this dung-heap, waiting for my comrades to take me off again."

"So, these two Heliers were the famous French Brothers?" the surgeon repeated, as he rose to take leave of his patient. "Bower, too, Mrs. Fleming's maiden name! I remember it well, and that her first husband ran through the old Sussex farmer's money, which she brought him as a marriage-portion, before he left the army to settle at the Grange. How strangely things come round! I dare say, a hundred other facts will occur to my recollection. But you have talked long enough now, and I have several visits to pay. Mind that you keep close, and I will send you word if there is any occasion for you to shift your quarters before La Belle Marie comes back."

He walked across the green to where his horse was fastened, making fresh annotations in his pocket-book as he went along. Whether he was recording any new symptom of his patient's malady, or the curious facts he had just heard, was very doubtful, since his interest in the cases he attended, and the circumstances incidentally brought to his knowledge, was about equal. Meanwhile, the seaman having managed, with the aid of his crutches, to hobble to the door, stood looking after the Doctor till he was out of sight; and then watched the flocks of geese on the sedgy pools, with his pale face turned towards the sea; from which direction, as the twilight closed in, the wind blew strongly.

CHAPTER XV.

As he rode across the stony waste to visit his outlying patients, Mr. Lawrence did not slacken his pace, though the track was a faint one. His sharp eyes knew every tint upon the weather-stained rocks, and each gleam which manifested itself where the low sunlight fell upon pools of water. Tregeagle might, according to old tradition, have been groaning over his uncompleted task of ladling out the fluid element with a limpet-shell, so hollow and unearthly were the shrieks and moans of the wind that swept over the desolate plain — not unlike the wail of a disappointed giant.

At last, the bridle-path struck the line of the public road, just where an inn, or halfway house, hung out its lights to attract travellers. It was a place frequented by miners and moormen, where many a quaint tale of Cornish tradition might be heard; but these were not new to the Camelford Doctor. Here, too, occasionally, a tourist or sportsman would put up for a night or two, submitting to mani-

fold inconveniences in order to cast a line in
the waters that descended from the hills, or to
wander through the wild scenery, rich in
mineral treasures and gloomy touches of Sal-
vator-like sublimity, existing to the artist's
eye in the savage heights of the great Tors,
and the deep, sterile valley that separated
Brown Willy from its yet more imposing
neighbour.

Mr. Lawrence gave his horse in charge to
the hostler, with many directions, to which the
man nodded assent.   He then made his way
into the inn, looking, as if it were a thing of
habit with him, at the superscriptions on the
luggage which the Bodmin coach had set
down that afternoon.   Without pausing, he
noted in his mind that a fire was burning in
the strangers' room, of which the door stood
open.   His visit to the sick child, whom he
was attending, did not last long.   Even for
a man of his hardy habits and daring courage,
it was getting to be a late hour for crossing
the moor; but still, before he remounted and
rode away, he knew as much as the landlord
could tell him of the stray guest who had
arrived by the coach, and was gone out with
his hammer to geologise.

The wind was singing a yet wilder melody now; grey clouds were hurrying on
before it, charged with rain; which, however,

had not yet begun to fall. The Doctor buttoned his overcoat tight across his chest. It was as unpleasant an evening for loitering as could well be imagined; and yet he stopped short when he heard, at a little distance, the tap of a hammer, and saw, seated on a heap of stones to the right of the track, the enthusiast in science who had taken up his quarters at the Jamaica Inn.

In his time, Mr. Lawrence had been a dabbler in most of the learned arts; and, in his museum at Camelford, specimens of the crystalline felspar, opaque and transparent mica, and grey quartz, which characterise the granite of the Bodmin range, as well as of the red lichen, *Lecanora perella*, which clings to the caverns and crevices of Row Tor, were to be seen, with many another remarkable production of nature; but he was quite at a loss to discover on what principle the stranger before him was making his selection.

Curiosity was a predominant feature in the character of the Camelford Esculapius; and the moment it struck him that the geologist was not acting in conformity with the acknowledged rules of science—that as he went on, more diligently than before, splitting the trumpery he had collected, he was, in fact, throwing away what was best worth retaining, and putting on one side what was absolutely worthless—Mr. Lawrence determined to get to the bottom of what certainly appeared to be an eccentric proceeding.

He rode nearer to the tourist, who was attired in a loose grey suit, admirably adapted for his occupation. He was so devoted to his employment that he did not look up from it, even when the hoofs of the Doctor's horse struck upon the flints close to his position— not until they stopped suddenly beside him.

"Good evening, Sir! Are you aware that there is a storm coming up from the west, and that the spot you have chosen for your scientific operations is about as ugly an one as a man could select, in which to be benighted? Let me advise you to return to your inn; you may find it difficult to do so an hour hence; and I doubt your discovering anything in that heap of rubbish to reward you for your trouble, and for the ducking to which you will be exposed, when those heavy clouds break in rain and thunder."

The stranger thanked him good-humouredly for his advice, and rose at once as if to depart, without taking the slightest heed of the mineral treasures which, a moment or two before, he had appeared to be laboriously collecting. As the Doctor looked in his face, which he did with his usual acuteness of observation, the instant it was turned towards

him, the features seemed not altogether unknown to him; but he could not immediately
recollect where he had lately seen that fair
though sunburned brow, on which the cap
was pulled low, the clear, blue, resolute eyes,
and firmly-cut mouth.

" The squall will pass over us. There
will be no rain to speak of on this side of
Brown Willy to-night," said the young man,
after surveying the sky attentively for an instant. " Still, I will so far profit by your
warning as to postpone farther inquiries into
the secrets of nature till daylight."

He laughed carelessly as he spoke, and
raised his cap as if in leave-taking, but the
Doctor did not ride away.

" You are well versed in the signs of the
weather," he said; " but perhaps you have
studied them on a different element. If I am
not mistaken, you have learned the lesson at
sea. Now, I was born within five miles of
Brown Willy, and I know, by the way he is
putting on his night-cap, that there will be
rain—yes, Sir, heavy rain—in less than an
hour. Time will show which of us is right."

" Well, then, the best thing you can do is
to ride fast to your home, wherever that may
be. You have probably farther to go than I
have," said the young man, quickening his
pace, as if willing to shake off his companion.

" I wish you good night, and a dry skin when
you get to your own gate."

" Our way is the same for a short distance, since I came out of my course to tell
you that the proper field for geological investi-
gations is the valley full of fragments, dry
bones, and fossils, which lies on the other side
of your inn.   You are wasting your time here.
If you will do me the honour to pay me a
visit, I will show you specimens of what is
really valuable—relics of past ages—mineral
ores ; in fact, everything that a man like yourself, if you are really a lover of science, would
most desire to see.   My museum at Camelford
has been the labour of a life—a labour of
love, too !   It would be a thousand pities if
you were to leave this part of the country
without seeing it."

He stooped down, as he spoke, and
handed a card to the stranger, who was
walking silently by his side, provoked at the
pertinacity with which his new acquaintance
had attached himself to him, but at heart too
much of the gentleman to repay his advances
with ungraciousness.

" I am only passing through the country,"
he said.   " To-morrow I may be gone.   I
fear that it will not be in my power to accept
your kind invitation."

" Young gentleman ! though you doubt

my skill about the weather (in proof of which
the rain is beginning to fall pretty thickly), I
shall bestow another piece of advice, unasked,
upon you—Never neglect an opportunity of
obtaining information. If it comes unsought,
so much the better; and do not be deterred
by its not appearing, at first, to be exactly of
the nature you require. I dare say there are
a score of things in my museum that would
interest you: yes, even if you were not as
fervent a votary of science as I am willing to
give you credit for being. A man does not
take up his quarters at the Jamaica Inn for
nothing. On the other side, after practising
for more than forty years in a neighbourhood,
riding hither and thither, rough and smooth,
one like myself, if fit for aught, must know
something of the district—of the riches the
earth carries in its bosom—of the population
born upon its soil, many of whom he has
ushered into the world, or striven heart and
soul, by day and night, to keep above its sod.
The chances are, I say, that a stranger seeking
information — be it of what kind it may—
might learn something from such a person.
But I see you are in a hurry, and the rain is
coming down pretty sharply, I wish you
good-night, Sir!"

The young stranger hesitated; his manner
changed; he extended his hand frankly, and

shook that of the surgeon, which was not withheld from him.

"I think I should like to see your collection," he said. "You are quite right in your opinion that the suggestions of an experienced philosopher and naturalist like yourself are not to be despised by a tyro in science, as I confess myself to be. You know that I am an ignoramus; I saw it in your first glance. At what time to-morrow shall I be most likely to find you at home? You are a busy man."

"Oh, come, come! your time is just as valuable as mine — perhaps more so, just now. Well, the later the better. Candle-light will do for the museum; mine are not daylight beauties. Any hour after sundown you will find me at my house in the High Street, at Camelford. Any one will show it to you, if you do not know it already; but I fancy you have, like myself, a quick eye, and it is right opposite to the inn at which the coach stops. I am certain you had the box-seat, when the Times changed horses at the King's Arms, last Thursday fortnight."

The young man nodded, but did not answer in words. The rain, pelting sharply in his face, proved the truth of his new friend's prophecy. Mr. Lawrence set himself firmly in the saddle, and rode away in the teeth of the blast, which blew more and more wildly.

He did not draw in his rein till the wet pavement of the town was under the hoofs of his good steed.

No one appeared to be sitting up for him, except the groom, who led the brown horse to his stable. There was, indeed, no woman residing in the house; for the surgeon held a firm conviction that the sex was not to be trusted, and he did not choose that feminine fingers should meddle with his curiosities. He always locked up his house, therefore, when he went from home, and put the key in his pocket. A light might now be seen burning over the door of the surgery, which was lower down the street, but the Doctor's dwelling was dark and silent. He undid the fastenings, fumbled about till he found a tinder-box of a more scientific construction than was common at that period, lighted a lamp, and went up-stairs.

His mind must have been running upon his museum; for he went into the rooms so called, which had once been attic chambers, but were now thrown into one long gallery, filled with the multifarious treasures he had brought together, and classed somewhat arbitrarily, and after a fashion of his own. No one but himself could have understood the meaning of the arrangement, which was governed, not by the nature of the objects,

but by the time and mode of their coming
into his possession. The Doctor's memory was
never at fault, and he was sure to have a tale
to tell, generally quite as singular in its way
as the rare plant or specimen to which it belonged, of the manner in which he had discovered each separate relic.

He had no one to speak to now ; but he
went silently and lovingly round the room,
slightly altering the position of some of his
mummies and skeletons, cases of minerals,
and Roman or British antiquities, as though
he were in expectation of a visitor to whom
he wished his really curious collection to be
shown to advantage. His next operation was
to make for himself, by means of a spirit-
lamp and a biggin, some intensely strong
coffee, the only beverage he ever drank ; and,
having provided himself with a quaint black-
letter book, containing an historical and de-
scriptive survey of his native county, he sat
up poring over its pages, until the first beams
of day streamed in upon him through the sky-
lights by which the museum was illuminated.

Then he extinguished his lamp, and, as
was his constant practice, went to his bed
just when the other dwellers in the quiet
little country town were beginning to move
about. One of his inveterate crotchets was,
that no man needed more than three hours'

sleep; and his was often broken, even during the short period he allowed himself for repose.

The Doctor opened the street door himself for his guest, when, at a somewhat late hour the following evening, the knocker was lifted with a gentler hand than the geologist had laid upon his hammer, when he sat tapping away at the rocks on the moor.

"Come in, come in! this way, if you please. Honour to science! I shall show you up to the museum at once. Everything is in order, and there is not a soul in the house but myself; no gossiping housemaids, or garrulous housekeeper to prate of your whereabouts. You can leave your cap below."

The young man laughed as he took his advice, hung his cap on a peg in the hall, and sprang up the stairs with a light, active step.

"A sailor, every inch of him!" said the surgeon, as he followed. "Not a bit like a philosopher or a naturalist—knew it at a glance. Besides, I had had a look at the craft before. How came you to be sailing under false colours, Lieutenant?"

"A matter of duty, in which every loyal subject is bound to assist me," said Osborne, gravely. "I am sent down here to collect information respecting the French schooner which carries on such a daring traffic on this coast. Now it strikes me that you are a person very likely to be able to obtain it for me."

"Can't say, exactly. Must not betray professional secrets—point of honour—silent as the grave. So you've a commission to execute touching La Belle Marie? She has not been in these waters this month past. What made you think of dropping anchor at the Jamaica Inn, of all places in the world?"

Osborne smiled at the Doctor's nautical phraseology. "You cure your patients too quickly," he answered. "When I found the nest, the bird was flown. In plain language, I had intelligence that the mate of the French schooner, having met with an accident, or caught a fever, which detained him after the sailing of the vessel, was in hiding among the bogs and morasses which lie between this town and Row Tor. With some difficulty, I traced him to his place of concealment, but I was a day too late; and the people who harboured him swear their lodger was as honest a fellow as ever breathed, and a patient of yours. He has evaporated, however, suddenly and suspiciously. Had you any reason to expect that he would depart so quickly, when you visited him yesterday?"

"Who can tell which way the wind may blow to-morrow? You a sailor, and not know that, after counting the hours for weeks,

lying idle in some stupid harbour, you hear it
in a moment, as it comes whistling among the
shrouds, from the very quarter whence you
have so long desired that it should blow! So
it is with a sick man's humour. To-day,
nothing can convince him that he is able to
walk a step. To-morrow, you hear that your
patient is off to market, or Helston Revel, or
gone back to his work at Wheal Maria. As
soon as that happens, if not before, I wash
my hands of him. His name is off my
books. Peace be to his ashes! Come, you
are neglecting the interests of science shamefully. Allow me to do the honours of my
museum."

On this point it was evidently useless
to question the Doctor. His professional
scruples were enlisted in behalf of his patient;
and it was far from impossible that the warning of impending danger, which had reached
the mate of La Belle Marie in time to prevent
Osborne's finding him at the farm-house on
the moor, came from his medical attendant.
The young Lieutenant walked slowly along
the gallery, looking, almost without seeing
them, at the various articles of *virtu;* and
listening, half unconsciously, to Mr. Lawrence's learned dissertations.

Meanwhile, a shrewd observer was watching his movements. Not one change of ex-

pression, not a single gesture of impatience,
escaped the surgeon's notice; and when Osborne stopped and took down from the shelf
a polished, blackthorn walking-stick, mounted
with silver, to which was attached a fragment
of discoloured, but once costly and delicate
lace, the Doctor remarked that his countenance altered; and that he with difficulty
controlled his agitation. As he held the stick
in his hand, his fair complexion flushed, and
a deep furrow contracted his forehead, while
he read the inscription.

"These ferns are remarkably curious,"
said Mr. Lawrence, coming close up to him,
and pretending to mistake the object which
his visitor was contemplating so intently.

"*Osmunda Regalis*, the royal flowering fern
—*Asplenium Adiantum Nigrum*, the Black
Maidenhair—Ah! you are wondering what
the connexion can be between these botanical
specimens and that Sussex thorn-cudgel; but
I have my own system of classification. Associations of time and place regulate the disposition of my treasures. These ferns were
gathered in the ravine at Woods, a place that
lay more in my beat formerly than it has
done of late years. Any quack, run-about
doctor, serves the turn of its present inmates.
Though a miserable sufferer from hypochon-
driacal disease, Mr. Helier does not seek re-

lief from the faculty. I dare say he is right! Physic is of little avail when the seat of the malady is in the mind. I have not been near the Manor-house for years: in fact, not since Lord Boscawen's last visit; and there is not much likelihood of my being called in to attend upon him there again. Though hale and hearty, his Lordship is past eighty, and resides entirely abroad.

" In physical strength, Sir, we are not to be compared with our grandfathers. Look at the steady lives men lead now, and think what was the existence of a person of fashion, when drinking and gaming were in vogue! Lord Boscawen is an instance of one who has trifled with his health and strength, so as to show that he must have a constitution of iron. He had a serious attack — a very serious one — at the time I allude to, five-and-twenty years ago. He took no care of himself; fever set in. The life he led was enough to kill him. He was never alone, if he could help it. His spirits were low, he said; it was impossible to live in such a dull place, without stimulants and company about him. The air of Woods, he declared, was death to him; he detested the place. When he was hipped and malcontent, I have seen him sit gazing at the red embers on the hearth, with his head full of fancies strong enough to turn them into shapes of terror. A fire had broken out at the Manor-house during a former visit, which affected his nerves in a way he never quite overcame. Some men have been haunted in the same manner all their lives, by a dread of robbers breaking into the house; the consequence of a fright in childhood. Lord Boscawen's monomania was the fear of fire. In his wild orgies he would turn pale, if he saw sparks flying about; and carelessness on this head among his domestics, who were a reckless band, was severely punished. There was always a watchman going round the passages at night; a page lay in his Lordship's room; and often, during his illness, have I ridden scores of miles on his best hunters to visit my patients, and return to sit up with him. Such was the shattered state of his nerves that he could not endure solitude. And yet, now, he is as well as ever he was in his life. He will live to be ninety, and see his descendants drop into the grave before him. Mark my words, Sir! he will survive all his grand-children, as he has done his sons and daughters."

"Forgive me, Sir," said Osborne, "but I was about to make an inquiry concerning this stick. It seems but an ordinary walking-staff. May I ask what made you consider it worthy of a place in your museum?"

" That stick? I shall arrive at it presently," said Mr. Lawrence. " It was speaking about the old house at Woods that led me into mentioning the circumstances under which his Lordship, as I was telling you, took an inveterate dislike to it. Though a free-thinker — perhaps, on that account — superstitious terrors beset him. He was out of health, and had unpleasant associations connected with a former residence at the Grange. In some shape or other—indigestion — nightmare — what you will—the familiar demon of the place, got possession of him. He was not fit to travel when he departed, but he was fairly driven away by broken rest and frightful dreams. When he left Woods, he gave his cousin, Captain Fleming, leave to live at the Manor-house, if—these were his words, not mine—'those damned ghosts would let him!' I never heard that any spirits but foreign brandy and other strong waters troubled poor Fleming. They did him harm enough, and after his death —a very tragical one—the place got a worse name than ever. I think I need not tell you the incidents connected with his untimely end. They were in every body's mouth at that time, and, though it is many years ago, the story is not forgotten. That staff was brought forward at Colonel St. Erme's trial, though not the instrument by which the murder, as it was pronounced to be, was alleged to have been committed."

Osborne looked up suddenly. His eyes met the clear, penetrating gaze of the surgeon.

"It was a case," he said, "which, as I have heard, rested entirely upon circumstantial evidence."

"Very true. I always thought that it was the absence of any other person to whom suspicion could reasonably attach, rather than sufficiently conclusive evidence against him, which led to Colonel St. Erme's conviction," said Mr. Lawrence. "It is a singular coincidence, but just before you came here this evening, I was looking at that stick which has attracted your attention so powerfully, and thinking that, if there were any of Colonel St. Erme's family now living, to whom it was important to establish his innocence (the old clergyman at Lezant and Miss Mary scarcely seem to belong to the real, tangible world) — if he had left a son, we will say — I might be disposed to depart from a rule I have laid down, and to make him the sharer of my knowledge of a very remarkable fact connected with this story of Fleming's murder, but which only came to my ears last night."

Osborne's agitation could no longer be concealed.

"Break through your excellent rule of caution for once," he said, "in my favour. I am most deeply interested in this question. At present, for professional reasons, I do not wish to lay aside my incognito; but less penetrating eyes than yours have seen through it. As soon as possible, all disguise shall be done away with. Be candid with me, I entreat!"

Mr. Lawrence still hesitated. "Well, I do not think it can do harm to tell you thus much. You must make out the links of connexion for yourself; perhaps I have led you to exaggerate the importance of the discovery. Fleming's widow — the poor weak woman who was Colonel St. Erme's supposed attraction to the Grange—after her husband's death married the farm-bailiff. This man, Jean Helier, I find, was one of the famous French Brothers, daring smugglers on the coast of Sussex, where he wooed and won the affections of Phœbe Bower, daughter of one of the Duke's richest farmers. She married Captain Fleming subsequently, and settled at Woods, whither her old lover seems to have pursued her. After the commotion caused by the murder and consequent proceedings subsided, this couple—these parted lovers—came together; but the circumstance of their former intimacy never transpired. This is all I can tell you, and I shall not give up my authority. Now then, if your inspection is over, I will offer you some coffee, and we will both lock up our professional secrets as carefully as I close my museum for the night."

While he spoke, the Doctor began to shut up his glass cases, and put away his coins and medals in their separate drawers. He half repented having diverged from his usual practice of confining his stores of information to his own breast, when he saw the effect produced by his confidential communication on young Osborne. As the blue, fiery eye lit, and the fair cheek flushed with eager animation, he traced the strong family likeness, not so much now to the dreamy, melancholy pastor of Lezant and his kinswoman, Mary St. Erme, as to her handsome father—the doomed exile.

"Ah! they are an unlucky race!" he said to himself, after letting his visitor out into the moonlit street. "The old Rector is as mad as a March hare, and the girl is scarcely sane. I dare say this young fellow will get

into a scrape, and perhaps lose his commission
—pretty nearly all he has, I fancy. What a
world it is! And what a fool you are, old
Lawrence, to be meddling and making with
what does not in the least concern you!"

In the deepest dell of the wooded ravine
which ran up into the coast, almost as far as
the old Manor-house, two hours before daybreak, next morning, a stirring scene was being
enacted. The officer of the Curlew had never
lost sight of the project he had formed to lay
hands on the other half of La Belle Marie's
cargo; and full powers had been entrusted to
him for carrying out his purpose. The men
who accompanied him were all strangers, and
neither friend nor foe had been admitted to his
confidence; but had the secret been guessed,
not all the drunken, riotous population of the
district, would have prevented the Lieutenant
carrying off his prize.

The red light of the lanterns fell upon the
cold clear stream that flowed over and under
the huge slab of slate that slanted across the
fall. The pale face of the young officer flushed
when he saw what a rich seizure had been
made, and he responded heartily to the wishes
of his zealous coadjutors that Jacob Mohr had
shared the fate of his goods. When the cave
by the waterfall had been completely cleared

of every cask and bale stored there by Lance
and his confederates, Richard drew off his
men ; and, leaving the spot to its almost un-
natural stillness, he walked beside the heavily-
laden wains, which, under a strong guard,
found their way through the country lanes to
the Court-house at Camelford.

END OF VOL. I.

LONDON:
STRANGEWAYS AND WALDEN, PRINTERS.
28 Castle St. Leicester Sq.

www.ingramcontent.com/pod-product-compliance
Lightning Source LLC
Chambersburg PA
CBHW060553030726
47498CB00005B/1370